THE
Sucker's
Teeth

Other Books By Joe Back

Horses, Hitches and Rocky Trails

by Joe Back

Mooching Moose and Mumbling Men

by Joe Back

The Old Guide Remembers

and

the Young Guide Finds Out

by Joe Back, with Vic Lemmon

THE
Sucker's
Teeth

Stories and Illustrations by

JOE BACK

JB

JOHNSON BOOKS

AN IMPRINT OF BOWER HOUSE

DENVER

Printed in Canada
Designed by Margaret McCullough
Illustrations by Joe Back

Library of Congress Control Number: 2019957272
ISBN 978-1-55566-480-0

10 9 8 7 6 5 4 3 2 1

Dedicated to the Buffalo Forks of the Snake River.

CONTENTS

List of Illustrations

Introduction

Joe Back was born April 12, 1899, in Montpelier, Ohio. His father was a country doctor who visited his patients by horse and buggy. A lover of horses, he maintained a breeding stable when not practicing medicine. Through him, Joe developed knowledge of horses at the earliest age, handling the buggy as his father made his rounds.

When Joe was only 9 years old his father died of a sudden heart attack. His mother relocated to California where she soon remarried. Joe could not get along with his stepfather who was quite a drinker; so when he got in trouble at school for drawing sketches of his 8th grade teacher, he decided that was enough of that whole situation and took off on his own.

Joe's mother had a cousin who managed the Fiddleback Ranch north of Douglas, so Joe headed there and was put to work as a choreboy for board and room. Having learned to handle horses from his father, he was soon promoted to full ranch hand status with wages of $45 a month.

With the onset of World War I, Joe entered the Navy. Proficient with firearms, he was assigned to be a machine gun instructor and the closest thing to an ocean he ever saw was Lake Michigan. Discharged in 1919, Joe returned to Douglas and began cowboying on the 55 Ranch for ranch foreman Wheeler Eskew. Wheeler was a top hand and Joe considered him "one of the finest men I ever got to know."

Joe had filed on a homestead 42 miles north of Douglas and had begun the improvements necessary to obtain full ownership when he heard about a big horse roundup. Hiring on with 6 or 8 other cowboys, they eventually caught several hundred stray horses, which were to be purchased by the Diamond G Guest ranch above Dubois. They then obtained a chuck wagon and rope corral and herded the horses from Douglas to Brooks Lake and the Diamond G, a distance of approximately 270 miles. The trip took 2 weeks and was filled with adventure.

The Diamond G wanted Joe to stay on as a wrangler and guide, so he leased the grass on his homestead and remained in the mountains.

He began guiding summer pack trips in the Teton Wilderness, including trips as far as Lewis Lake in Yellowstone National Park. In the fall, he would guide elk, deer, and bighorn sheep hunters.

Joe Back had always liked to draw and sketch and the Brooks Lake country was full of subject material. He began making sketches of horses, mountains, and cowboys and gave them away to ranch guests. One summer-long guest was Louis Agassiz Fuertes, a staff artist with National Geographic. When he saw Joe's sketches, he encouraged him to attend the Art Institute of Chicago.

Initially rejected because he had only completed the 8th grade, Joe figured that was the end of that idea. But when Fuertes found out about it, he gathered up Joe's sketches and sent them to the Institute with a strongly worded letter; Joe was accepted. He quickly sold his homestead and headed east. It was at the Art Institute of Chicago that Joe would meet his future wife and lifelong partner.

Mary Waters Cooper was born on Dec. 3, 1906 in Minneapolis, Minnesota. While still an infant, her father moved the family to Vermont. Even as a young child, Mary's interests in nature and art were evident. Her notebooks would be festooned with drawings, often of plants or animals. Her father was a member of the Green Mountain Club, which established hiking trails reaching to Canada, so Mary spent weekends hiking the hills and clearing trails. Early pictures show Mary with various animals, including several pet snakes.

Graduating from high school at the age of 16, Mary was admitted to Berea College in Kentucky. A small, prestigious school, Berea charged no tuition but required students to hold jobs at the college. When Mary arrived, she brought one of her pet snakes which caused quite a commotion and was eventually placed in the biology lab.

While Mary was at college, her family relocated to Chicago. Joining them there following graduation, she began taking classes at the Art Institute of Chicago. Classes in animal anatomy were held at the Field Museum of Natural History, and one day while Mary was sketching animals, someone walked up behind her and remarked, "That's a helluva good bear!" It was Joe Back.

Joe courted Mary during 1931 and 1932, and they finally married in February of 1933, during the great depression. Jobs were scarce, but Joe was hired as a foreman by the National Park Service for $175 a month, and Mary was appointed to run a trailside wildlife museum for $100 per month. They lived on Joe's salary and saved Mary's earnings with a plan to move to Wyoming.

In the spring of 1935, Joe and Mary bought a 1927 Buick to make the trip west. They sewed a canvas tent which could be affixed to the side of the car and camped their way through the country, arriving at Dubois, Wyoming, Joe's old stomping ground.

Moving to the high country, Mary and Joe purchased the abandoned and dilapidated Lava Creek Ranch. Working nearly round the clock, they rendered the ranch cabins ready for winter. And that first winter was a tough one with deep snow and cold temperatures. Joe would take 2 days to snowshoe the 22 miles to Dubois for the mail and a few groceries. But they both decided to stick it out.

Given her somewhat genteel and urban background, it is amazing how much Mary took to Wyoming's wildlands. Her sentiments are perfectly reflected in a short essay to the Berea College alumni newsletter, where she spoke of her first winter in the wilderness.

"Sheer beauty. It is a privilege to just be in a world so lovely, so bright with changing color; so rich in the detail of bird and animal form and action, and the patterning of the lodgepoles and the willows; so tremendous in the massing of the great mountains; so aloof and remote from the smoke and fussiness of human crowding."

Then later, "There is a relief to all one's senses at the lessened feeling of being just a cog in a great, impersonal, and intricate Society, the relief and responsibility of being "on your own" for better or for worse."

And in closing, "I have actually heard this vivid, beautiful, ever-changing country called "God-forsaken." We both find it in our hearts to thank God that it is so comparatively human-forsaken."

Mary and Joe ran the Lava Creek Ranch as a dude outfit for nearly 4 years. These were lean times, calling for improvisation and doing it yourself. Mary learned to do carpentry, dig ditches, butcher elk, and skin beaver. During the fall, Joe would be gone for weeks on end guiding hunters, and in her journals Mary speaks of how lonely she became without him; truly an inseparable pair.

They later sold Lava Creek Ranch and bought the Rocker Y, another dude ranch, but a bigger operation. While they loved the lifestyle, it did not allow them the time they needed to pursue their art careers. After a long day in the saddle or a day spent cooking and cleaning, their creative energies for painting and drawing were diminished.

During World War II, Joe and Mary worked for the war effort in California; Joe as a shipyard welder, and Mary as an airplane mechanic. Returning to Dubois at the war's end, they dude ranched for one more year.

By the spring of 1946, Joe and Mary came to realize that they would never become full-time artists running a hectic dude outfit. They sold the Rocker Y, moved east of Dubois and built a cabin that would also serve as an art studio.

Drawing and sculpting did not pay all the bills, so Joe took odd jobs, including stints with the Wyoming Game and Fish Department as a seasonal game warden and packing fish into the wilderness for stocking. He also continued guiding hunters and always got his own elk for the winter's meat - a staple since the Lava Creek days.

Joe published a small pamphlet on horse packing, "How to Tie a Diamond Hitch" illustrated with his colorful sketches. It was in big demand, so he launched a book project to produce a "horse packer's bible." The end product was *Horses, Hitches and Rocky Trails*, still in print and considered one of the best guides to horse packing in existence. His last chapters advocate respecting the wilderness and keeping care of the mountain country. He would later publish several other books, and Mary would publish *Seven Half-Miles From Home*, a reminiscence of her walks in the upper Wind River country.

The University of Wyoming asked Mary to teach extension art classes, and she was soon teaching in Dubois, Lander, Crowheart and

Riverton. Her classes were immensely popular, and the annual art show she arranged for her students and regional artists gave rise to the Wind River Valley Artists' Guild. Her efforts were later recognized when she received the Governor's Award for Service to the Arts. In addition, both she and Joe were awarded the Medallion of Honor by Central Wyoming College in 1982.

The Backs celebrated their 50th wedding anniversary in 1983, and over 200 people arrived at their small studio home. This turnout portrayed the public's appreciation for all of Joe and Mary's community service.

Joe Back passed away on September 7, 1986. This was a terrific blow to Mary - she had lost her husband, best friend, and lifelong partner in all affairs. Despite the loss, Mary continued her work with the Wind River Valley Artists' Guild and maintained her habit of walking and bird watching along the Wind River; but she had lost much of her desire to paint with Joe's passing.

Mary Back died on May 28, 1991, but the legacy of Joe and Mary Back lives on through their artwork, writings and in the fond memories of countless friends.

The Wind River Valley Artists' Guild is now housed in the beautiful Headwaters Arts and Conference Center in Dubois. Visitors can enjoy the artwork of Joe and Mary Back as well as many other fine artists.

Joe and Mary Back were inducted into the Wyoming Outdoor Hall of Fame in 2013.

—Courtesy of Wyoming Game & Fish Department

The wrangler rode into sight.

A Foreword About Tusk Hunters

One of the last wild refuges of the American elk is away up high in northwestern Wyoming, a strange and wonderful upland called the Buffalo Plateau. This massive upthrust is over eleven thousand feet high, and large enough to affect the weather. It rears up and splits the storms, so that Wind River Valley southeast of it enjoys a relatively mild climate. It's wild, cliffy, and untamed, yet it contains many peaceful meadows, with great sweeps of timber following down the network of streams rushing from the enormous arctic uplands. After calving in the valleys below, many families of elk head for this lush paradise, there to stay until late fall and early winter storms force them to the lower valleys.

This is horse country—no roads, no jeeps—and hard to get into. Winter snows pile up from ten to fifteen feet. Streams radiate from it to water much of our continent: the Buffalo Forks to the Snake, to the Columbia, to the Pacific; and the Yellowstone, Shoshone, and Wind Rivers by way of the Missouri and Mississippi to the Gulf of Mexico.

Stangely enough, you can't see this magnificent plateau. Nowhere, away from it, does it dominate the skyline. It is not celebrated in song or story. It is a strong and secret refuge in the hearts of those who know it, and knowledge of it forms a bond between strangers.

Most of the story in *The Sucker's Teeth* is based in the lower reaches of the Buffalo Forks of the Snake River: South Fork, Soda Fork, and North Fork. As this story is twisted up with people versus teeth and a few other things, I think some explanations are needed about the trouble a lot of elk had with some of their teeth, and *this* is not fiction.

Some folks say that a scamp, a scalawag, and a scoundrel are three stages of the same thing, and that the latter had to start in on the ground floor to attain the final qualifications. But it seems in most of the professional tusk hunters of Jackson Hole had graduated at the head of their class without any first grade preliminaries.

There wasn't very many of these corrupt sinners or we wouldn't have any elk left now. You'd think that anyone who would kill a wapiti or American elk for just two of his teeth had sold his soul to the devil. For in the days before the turn of the century, and for some

1

In 1926, I was a horse wrangler for a hunting outfit, making my first trip into this part of Jackson Hole. Many times since then I've worked for different outfits, traveling through this section. I hope my last trip is still ahead of me. In this story of *The Sucker's Teeth*, the characters are suggested by people I know now or knew then. All names are fictitious and the plot is pure fiction. The country and the life are real.

My friend, if you would like to join Shorty Beel and Buck Bruen's club, just keep turning the pages.

Yours truly,

Joe Back
Dubois, Wyoming

Chapter One

Vince saddled up and rode out early that morning to hunt the horses. The big spruce had wrecked two or three sections of buck fence when it fell over dead, and the horses found the hole before we did. I had just got the last poles spiked tight on the repair job when I heard Pete's Democrats set up an infernal braying. It was a half mile up to the corrals, but the racket sure carried through the timber. When I heard the story of my wife, Velma's troubles at the ranch, I knew those mules must be psychic.

Vel was just stoking up the kitchen range to start dinner when she saw a car drive up in front of the bunkhouse. A thickset man got out, and as he looked around, Vel thought she recognized him as a deputy sheriff from the county seat 75 miles below Roaring River. When she opened the kitchen door, the man with the badge and the big hat saw her and said, "Hi, Mrs. Thompson." Just then the wrangler rode into sight, driving some loose horses ahead of him toward the open gate of the corral.

"Before I could say a word, the sheriff said, 'Excuse me a minute,' and took off toward the corrals. Pretty soon he came back into sight, with Vince walking alongside. He was waving his hands around talking, and the sheriff was shaking his head." It wasn't an election year, and Velma said she couldn't figure it out. "Vince went into the bunkhouse, and the deputy came over and started explaining. 'Sorry, but I've gotta take Vince with me, Mrs. Thompson.' He waved a folded paper at me. He said, 'I've known Vince since he was a kid. Good boy, except he goes on a binge once in a while. Coupla months ago he went on a party. When he come outa' th' haze and found he was married to a tramp, he took a look around an' pulled out.' He shook his head and waved the paper. 'She got out a warrant for wife desertion, and poor Vince has gotta face th' music.' When Vince came out of the bunkhouse with his bedroll, he came over to say goodbye, and *then* those darned mules started up the darndest hullaballoo I ever heard.

"After the sheriff left with Vince," Velma said, "I was just dishing up for a lonely dinner when you showed up, Bill, just in time for the bad news. No, the sheriff wouldn't stay for dinner. He said he and

5

Vince would eat in Roaring River." Velma went over to the stove to dish up more food. "Vince asked me to tell you he was sorry to put you in the hole, to have to get another horse wrangler. Well, I gave poor Vince a check for the time he had coming, so I guess that's that."

While we finished dinner, we were wondering how Pete Elaby was doing with his ulcerated tooth. This was the visiting dentist's day in Roaring River. "He should be back tonight," Velma said, "Hope he gets over to the store. I gave him a big list of stuff we need." We got up from the table, and were still talking about where could we locate another good horse wrangler, when those jacks down to the corral started to bray. Velma went over to a kitchen window. "Maybe that's Pete now. Hope it's not another sheriff," she was saying, when Moocher the collie started up a frenzied barking out in front of the ranch house. A loud car horn started to compete with the mules and the dog, so Vel and I hurried to the front door. As I opened the door, I could see that the driver's brains didn't match none with his big car. The shiny new car, close to the front porch, was gouged into the fringe of Velma's delphiniums she had worked so hard on. The fat man behind the wheel stopped blaring the horn when he saw us come out on the porch. I shushed Moocher under the porch, but those angry growls should have warned me. The dog had a dang sight more insight than I ever will.

As the portly figure grunted out of the car, Velma noticed the *Kansas* on the front license plate, and figured out just who this was. "By gravy, if I'd known what a crummy lookin' outfit. . ." He stopped short when I waltzed over. "If you don't like what you. . ." I was just about to go whole hog when Vel jabbed me in the ribs with a "Sh! Sh! Take it easy, Bill." Then I remembered who this rhino could be. O yeah, the hunter list. Big wheat farmer—biggest, he wrote. More subsidy than any other in Kansas—big talk—lotsa letters. Paid only part of the earnest money down. O yeah—wait 'n' see—yeah. Well, the loud-talking hunter finally got settled in our strongest chair at the dining table. While he was cramming down Vel's fine vittles he kept rolling his eyes at the trophies I had hung on the log walls. As he puffed and panted his food down, he kept mumbling comments under his breath.

Every once in a while he would shift his weight around and adjust the long, bayonet-sized hunting knife attached to the straining belt of the barrel-sized middle. While I sat in a chair waiting for the man to finish his meal. I noticed the wheat baron suspiciously examined each dish Velma set before him. Finally he heaved to his feet.

6

"Well, Thompson, I come early, I admit, I sorta wanted ta see what I was gettin' inta. An' now that I'm here I might as well go through with th' hunt. Your rates are O.K., and I would. . ." I had to interrupt him. "I can't take you out to camp for a few days. Guides won't be here for a coupla days. Be tomorrow or next day." I told Kansas we could put him in a cabin and feed him till then.

After he drove his car around to a newly built cabin, I helped the fussy guy unload enough equipment for six hunters. Just as I stacked his last three heavy gun cases in a corner. I saw this lovable character turn back Velma's prized Hudson Bay blankets. He was thumping the new mattress and springs on the rustic bed frame. The fire I'd built in the stove was starting to warm up the cabin, so I figured the mighty hunter was settled. "Mr. Long," I says, just recollecting his name, "supper is at six and breakfast is at seven o'clock. In the meantime, if you need anything, just holler."

Long hadn't heard me. He was busy rubbing at a label that had been left on a window frame, and was mumbling half to himself, "By gravy, if I had this place I'd. . . Oh, yes, Thompson, I think I'll make out. Uh, thanks."

Well, I was sure glad to be leaving, so I grabbed the door knob and started out. Velma dang near ran over me as she came in, kinda red-faced, with a mop and a dustpan. "Oh, Bill, I haven't yet had time to get the shavings and sawdust cleaned up. If you'll show Mr. Long around the ranch, I'll tidy up the cabin." As we left the cabin, and Velma started to lift a heavy leather bag out of her way, I saw Long give her a suspicious look.

We were just starting down toward the corrals when Pete Elaby drove up in the pickup. After Pete got out I introduced him to Long. The grinning packer stuck his hand out to the reluctant farmer. "Glad t'uh know yuh, Mr. Long!" Long quickly dropped Pete's hand, and peered up at the black eye and swollen jaw. So I put in my two cents' worth. "Didja get it pulled, Pete, or who hit yuh? A bad tooth is no cinch in this frosty weather."

Pete rubbed his face and grinned, "That dentist pulled it, Bill. Now mebbe we can git some work done." When Long heard that, he mumbled something about going back up to his cabin for a camera, so Pete and I kept on walking down toward the corral.

We worked till dark stopped us. We turned out the horses and mules, and kept the bell mare and couple of wrangle horses on hay in the corral for the night. I'd forgotten about the grumpy hunter till we went past his lighted cabin on our way to the ranch. "Looks like your friend knows how to operate a gas lamp," Pete says. "I'll bet he had t'find out from Velma." I wasn't very happy about this bird, anyhow. By the time we had stoked up and were feeling spry, Vel told us that Mr. Long had eaten supper with very little comment and gone back to his cabin.

Moocher started to bark outside as a car drove in and stopped at the back porch. When we heard voices and a knock at the kitchen door, Velma cried, "It's Sally! I'm sure glad she could come," and opened the door. "Oh, Sally, I'm sure happy you could get off the job to help us for hunting season."

Sally Sublette and her brother-in-law, Tom Hoster, ate supper, while we sat around and jawed about all the news down on the reservation. They were Shoshone friends of ours. Sally, a small, pert Indian girl, had worked for Velma several summers. Last spring she graduated from college. Now she was working in the office at the post. While Sally and Vel washed up the dishes and got all the women-jabber outa their systems, we got Sally's bags outa Tom's car. Tried to get Tom to stay all night. But he said he was right in the middle of haying and had to git back to the ranch.

Sally Sublette was serving breakfast to Long the next morning. He got up late, and his sulky manners irritated the sweet-tempered Shoshone. Pete and I ate early and were down at the corrals. Pete was shoeing one of his mules and I was squatted down in the saddle shed fixing a latigo on a pack saddle when Velma squeaked open the corral gate. "If you don't take that . . . that . . ." she looked at the mule tied to a corral pole, "that jackass hunter out to camp or run him off the place," she was shaking, "I'll . . . c-crown him with my worst frying pan.

"This . . . this Long character told Sally to take back that ham and eggs and serve him something fit to eat." Vel was livid with rage. "He said he didn't like foreigners to be cooking his food anyway!" I throwed that good pack saddle down and stomped out of the corral. I could hear Vel panting along behind me. I heard Pete shut the gate I forgot, and by the time I got up to the big subsidy standing by his car, dang if one of them jacks didn't start to hee-haw.

Maybe there's no money in getting peeved, but I wasn't that broke when I whirled the wheat man around and grabbed him by the wrist. "Look here, you fat farmer, if you don't go an' apologize t' Sally, I'll beat your dumb head off." He had his expensive rump backed up against that car, and was bulging his eyes at me. I could hear Vel behind me swearing college words under her breath. I hadda notion

8

to bust him one anyhow, and then he got to stuttering, "Wa-wa-wait a minute, Mr. Thompson. I uh, I uh, I can see I was in th' wrong. I uh, I uh, wasn't feeling too good this morning."

Well, Long waddled over to the kitchen, with us right behind him. He made his apologies to Sally, adding, "To be truthful, Miss Sublette, that was the finest breakfast I've had in a long time." His ruddy face flushed some more and he stammered, "Yuh know, I-I, haven't been well, and I uh, I been outa sorts lately."

Well, I thought, this oughta be tailgate for this hunter, but he went over to his cabin and didn't show any sign of pulling his freight, so I figgered his hide was thicker'n any moose I ever skinned. Later on, Pete and I came up for coffee. Velma was checking over the camp lists and Sally was kneading up a big batch of bread dough in a dish pan. They stopped and had a mug with us.

The packer sipped some coffee and said, "Bill, I figgered when I was sittin' on the corral pole watchin' th' show, I'd get to see guide hide an' wheat grains scattered all over th' landscape, but I got fooled." Pete reached over to pinch off a piece of dough, and Sally turned a worried eye on him. He started to chew it, rolling his eyes at the roof logs. "Nope, it's O.K., Sally. If it was his wheat it couldn't taste that good."

Well, that crack cleared the air. I asked Sally, "Heard from Johnnie lately?" She looked pleased. "Sure have, Bill. John writes me a letter nearly every month. Sometimes two." Pete, his face still swelled, looked like he was having a hard time swallowing his coffee. "Shorty told me, out at camp, that that boy Johnnie'll be the best dentist Roaring River ever saw, when he sets up his office next year. Even if he is Shorty's nephew, I wish he coulda fixed this tooth."

We went down to the corrals, and passing Long's cabin I told Pete, "I gotta notion ta run that sap head off th' place. If I hadn't made a deal for that land down below, I wouldn't need cash that bad." Elaby opened the gate and grinned. "Sometimes, Bill, yuh gotta take th' bitter with th' sweet. Winter's a comin'." "Yeah, sure is, Pete." I was still sore about the wheat magnate. "Callin' Sally uh foreigner! Why, hell, Pete, th' Indians was in the mountains thousands a years before the whites stole 'em from 'em. We're th' foreigners, and that subsidy-grabbin' jackass is the worst of us." That packer put his paw on my shoulder, he says, "Look here, pardner, *don't* insult my mules."

Velma and Sally were busy packing panniers full of food and other supplies. The list that Shorty, out at camp, had made was a big one. In the next two or three days another guide or two were due, besides, three more hunters were due in. Elaby and yours truly were busy getting his mules and the ranch horses shod up and figured out. The barn and saddle shed was stacked with equipment. The log store house looked pretty empty. We had tents, tarps, and other gear strung around on the hitch rack and corral poles. Our fingers were sore from sewing rips and repairing holes left from last season's use.

Long showed up with a camera, and took a lot of pictures of the activity around the place. He made half-hearted friendly comments, and asked questions about the game conditions, and life in the surrounding mountains. He seemed to be most concerned about the camp, and especially the cook. I told him about Shorty.

Elaby grinned at my picture of Shorty. "By hell, Bill," he says when Long left, "if this grain king ever *does* get ta camp, ol' Shorty'll cut him down ta size. If he gets poppity with *that* cook, there'll be a lot less wheat raised in Kansas."

The rest of the busy day was pretty tranquil. The noon meal and supper seemed to agree with Long, and his friendly overtures were accepted in kind and returned by everybody. Nearly everybody. Sally said that evening, "I've noticed Mr. Long several times trying to pet Moocher. But you know that dog is smarter than I thought. He just isn't having any."

After breakfast next day I drove the pickup, loaded with split wood, up close to the woodpile stacked against the kitchen wall. I was going to Roaring River that morning to try and locate a new horse wrangler. I heard a noise as I was stacking the last of the wood, and it was the fat hunter starting to talk. He had reverted to his natural aplomb. "Thompson," he started out with, "if you'll come over to the cabin I'd like to have a talk with you."

Now, I'm not as cagey as some, but I had a hunch there was a Kroochef deal he'd figured out; but I followed Subsidy into the cabin anyhow. He goes over to the chair by the stacked up leather cases and sits down. He says, real gracious like, "Set down, Bill, set down." Long pursed up his thin lips at the ceiling, thinkin' like, then he reached over to a carved leather case on the polished table top and took out a bottle and a couple glasses. When he started to pour, I held up my hand. "Whoa, now, Mr. Long. All right f'r you or anybody else. But leave me out. I never touch the stuff. I don't hold against it, but me, I'm a teetotaler." Long nodded amiably and put the cork back in the bottle. He leaned back in his chair, holding the brimming glass up to the sunlit window. As he squinted through the amber liquid, he hummed contentedly.

10

Then he starts. "You know, this country is plenty rugged, and it takes a rugged man to hunt here." Long took a loud sip of whiskey and drummed his pudgy fingers on the table top. He pursed up his lips, and kind of gives me one of them loan shark smirks I've read about. You know, board of directors, the magazines say.

About then, I got to looking around at the boxes, cases, and bags stacked around the cabin. Looked like a sporting goods and gun crank's paradise: three big gun cases, hand carved, a couple pair of field glasses with leather scabbards, two long hunting knives, camp axes on belts, cartridge cases, and a long kind of spy glass with shiny tripod. There was a couple rolled-up sleeping bags and some leather-ended canvas sacks, besides several big leather bags about the size of a washtub. And when I saw the folding table and chairs and that collapsible toilet, I got sorta dizzylike. Somehow I got to thinking about Pete loading that stuff on his long-eared playmates, and about the tent this jerk would have to have out in camp. I reckon the buzzing I heard was Long talking, but I couldn't listen for wondering what kind of a six-legged horse to put him on, and if I could locate a two-headed guide to nurse him around the hills. All this time, Big Wheat musta been talking. Mebbe this *was* a dream, but when I finally got my dumb peepers focused on the mortgage factory sport with the silverplated "where-am-I" pinned to his shirt front, I come outa the haze. I damn well knew what was coming next.

As the man droned on about "what a nice set-up," I could feel a sorta cold sweat coming on; and when my mane hair started to tip my hat brim down onto my forehead, I could see through the glass. But the frame looked wrong. The money he'd paid down was only half in earnest, but winter was coming.

A few years ago, about the time hunting season started, I got a letter that still riles whatever principles I think I've got. The writer wrote that he, upon arriving at my ranch, would pay a stated sum for a couple of fresh elk and deer carcasses, dressed clean and hung up, at the writer's convenience. The letter also said that he, the under-signed, was a very close-mouthed individual, and that I had a very high recommendation from intimate friends, *and* he wished a very early reply, etc., etc.

Well, I know that us hillbillies haven't got a rep for being too bright, and mebbe I wasn't up front either. But if some star-polishing credit manager thought he could pin a poacher sign on this chicken, it would take more dinero than this floured-up numbskull could get hold of. But I got to feelin' about then that I hadn't been any too well lately,

11

I musta went Berkshire.

and that I'd been outa sorts besides. When I come outa that trance, I heard some snatches of what Mr. Long was saying. "And so, Thompson, if you will have one of your men, or you yourself bring in a nice bull elk and a good buck deer, I will pay . . ."

Well, you know, about then I was damned *sure* I hadn't been too well lately; and I knew I was *sure* outa sorts, when I jumped up and started to throw out them big gun cases and all the shiny hardware and carved leather gear outa that dad-burned contaminated cabin.

Well, sir, I musta went Berkshire, cause when I come to, I was sure there musta been some hella-ballo. I was standing outside leaning against the cabin wall, with Velma holding her hand on my briskit. I heard a car starting up close by, and there was that Kansas hunter driving past the bunkhouse. He had them big hunting glasses hung on an open car door handle, and leather cases jumbled up in plain sight on the dang seats. Velma had a rolling pin in her hand, and was laughing her fool head off. I looked around at somebody inside the cabin, and saw Sally sweeping up some broken glass on the dad-burned scratched-up floor. There wasn't much derbish around to show any subsidy had been left. Just as that big car started to speed up, I saw Pete gallop up on that big sorrel horse of his. He had a big grin on his lop-sided jaw. About then, them dang jacks down at the corral started the blamedest racket I ever heard. And then Moocher quit barking.

Everybody had different stories about what happened, but the main thing was, when the laughing got down to giggles, I was in the pickup headed for town to look for a horse wrangler and to get the mail.

Chapter Two

Good thing I had my ears lowered, because I met up with a man named Slim Wilson in the barber shop. Later he turned out to be a first class hand. About 45 years old. A fine wrangler and a good packer. By the time he had his bed, war bag and saddle loaded in the pickup, and had the mail and other stuff piled in, we were ready to go home.

"Slim, you mind drivin' this chariot?" I wanted to look over the mail. "Not atall, Bill, just tell me when ta turn off." Slim, I could see, was a good driver, so I got to reading what letters I'd got. Saw that I'd have to do down to the railroad at the county seat: Smithers, a hunter we'd had out last year was due in today. Well, I'll go tomorrow. Some more letters and lotsa bills. Mail for Hackett, the hunter out in our camp, and some more. Looks like those two friends Dr. Forrester and Mr. Parsin are going to show up in a day or so. From their letter they sound like fine people to hunt with. Well, I wasn't any help to Slim while I was going over the mail, but I did tell him some about our ranch and camp setup. He talked like he had plenty savvy about the life, but he was no phonograph.

Finally, when Wilson wheeled in to the ranch, I could see we had more company. A car was standing by the kitchen door, and I could see Velma talking with three men close by.

Naturally I hadn't told Slim Wilson about our big recent hunter, but Slim looked at me sorta sharp when I mumbled, "I hope these birds don't raise wheat!" When Slim stopped the outfit and we got out, I was relieved to recognize Tim Smithers, the big broker from New York. The other men turned out to be George Parsin and Dr. Forrester. I felt like a new man.

We shook hands all around, and everybody got acquainted. At our place we're not fancy. Everybody eats at the big table, old-fashioned ranch style, when we're operating. That Subsidy didn't know what he missed, but was he human?

Smithers wanted to know about "his old pal, Shorty: Mrs. Thompson, I'll bet Shorty learned how to cook from you, haw, haw!" Smithers had everybody laughting when he told about Shorty and the guides out in camp last year. "Best time in my life . . . best food

14

and best country . . . Been planning on it ever since last fall," etc.
He asked about Tony Belknap, who wrangled and packed last year.
"Leg broke? Well, well. Gotta watch them horses, haw, haw."
Forrester was a thin, gangly M.D. from Indiana. His friend George
Parsin, formerly from Indiana, now with a museum, in New York,
was a naturalist. Both were genial, friendly men, easy to get along
with. "We drove out, taking out time. Lots of movies on the trip."
Parsin said he was sure going to use a lot of film in hunting camp.
"We met Tim this morning in the hotel, and when we found he was
coming up here, he took a chance on two wild drivers." "Haw, haw!"
(Smithers hadn't changed from last year). "That'll cost you a good
picture of Shorty and me, George, haw, haw!"
    The way these hunters were getting acquainted seemed to me a good
sign. The first hunters we'd had out at the season's start had been an
easy going bunch. They were fine hunters and good sports. Those
men were back home by this time with their trophies and meat. Hackett,
out in camp now, was kind of a stuffy sort, but it was Shorty and
Buck who were stuck with him. Now it looked like we had three
hunters again that were going to be as fine to get along with as those
first. I thought of the slim hunting equipment these men had unloaded.
"Just brought the needfuls," Dr. Forrester said, "too much is a damn
bother." "Haw, haw!" Tim Smithers laughed about what "junk" he
came with last year.
    That evening, while I was visiting and talking over game conditions
and camp with the hunters, Slim Wilson was visiting with Pete Elaby
over by the big stove. Elaby was showing the wrangler a rawhide
hackamore he was working on. Smithers and I were listening to Forrester and Parsin describe some happenings on their hunt in Alaska
last year. I hadn't heard any car drive up, and didn't know there was
a caller, until I saw Pete walk over to the door. As he opened it, a
game warden we both knew came in. He said, "Hi, everybody," then
he happened to look over at Slim Wilson. Wilson was standing side-
ways to the warden in the shadow under the gas lantern hanging from
a roof log. He seemed to be making an intent examination of the
headstall on the colorful hackamore. The game warden took off his
hat and smiled around at the crowd, then he walked over to Wilson
and stuck out his hand. "Why, hello, Slim." The new wrangler flitted
a glance over in my direction. Then he quickly shook hands, said,
"Hi, warden," with little enthusiasm, sorta nodded, and sat down to
look at the hackamore. The game man gave Wison a queer sort of
squint, and then I introduced Kompton to the hunters.

15

After we'd chewed the fat about this and that, he asked me in a low tone if we could have a few words in private, so I excused myself to the hunters. Velma and Sally were slicking up the kitchen for the night, and outside of friendly greetings, paid no attention to us as we sat down at a corner table.

"Bill, a hunter from Kansas showed up at my place this afternoon," Kompton had a cold left-handed grin as he said this. "Claims you're a crook." Warren Kompton had a reputation as a fine game warden and a square shooter, but the thoughts of Long began to get my dander up. He went on, "Says you throwed him off the place, after you'd signed him up and taken his earnest money." I stewed that over, and told him, "O.K., Warren, I'll admit all but the crooked part. Now let's hear what else this bird has on me."

"All right, Bill, here she goes," Kompton said in a disgusted tone. "He said your food and service is horrible, your cabins not fit for a dog, and if your camp is run like your ranch, we oughta take away your outfitter's license."

No dishes rattled and no water sloshed for quite awhile. It was very quiet in the kitchen, when I saw the game warden staring up past me with an unbelieving look on his weatherbeaten face. When the smoldering cigarette fell out of his gaping mouth, I shoved back to get up out of my chair. To brace myself, I started to put one hand on the table. Looking up into the ferocious glare that little Shoshone gal of ours had riveted on Kompton, I put my hand on the - ah - sticky bleeding scalp of the wheat magnate.

When Sally cried out, "He pinched me," I come to. Looking down, I saw I had flattened out those slender brown fingers clutching a hot and soapy dishrag. Then that pretty little savage leaned over toward the dismayed game warden and burst out agin, "He pinched me, and that isn't all he did—that horrible man from Kansas!"

I didn't know whether to laugh or cuss. I happened to look over at the dining room door, and there was Pete Elaby's bony, freckled mug grinning past the tall horse wrangler. I don't know how *much* Slim had heard; anyhow, he was staring at me with accusing eyes. I started to look around for Velma. Just then, the jittered game warden gave a choky sort of grunt, and began to clutch frenziedly at his shirt pocket. His pain-contorted face—plucking fingers—could mean a bad heart, we all must have thought at the same time.

The small table overturned, as Wilson, Elaby and I made a grab for Kompton, to ease him down on the floor. He yelped, "Wait, wait, cigarette, cigarette." He was pinching at his pocket. The small wisp

The ferocious glare of the little Shoshone.

of smoke from his shirt pocket didn't have a chance. A big dipper of
soapy water changed all that. Velma had pushed the little Shoshone
warrior aside and put out the fire.

"That must have been a good one. Haw, haw, haw! Ol' Shorty
shoulda been here. Haw, haw, haw!" Smithers stood in the doorway,
with Dr. Forrester and Mr. Parsin, grinning at the jumbled-up show
in the kitchen. I could see Velma with her arm around Sally, standing
over by the big wood stove. Vel was smiling as she talked in a low
voice to Sally. Sally, with one hand over her mouth, was staring,
big-eyed, at the amused crowd. By the time we got a bunch of salve
plastered on the game warden's burn, I began to think this was getting
to be a ding-danged opry house instead of a ranch. Kompton looked
down with a sad grin at his ruined red shirt. Suddenly Pete Elaby
reached down to fumble around under the sink. He came up with
Warren's scratched-up badge. "Do you reckon you'll need this, Warden?" Kompton sheepishly reached for it. "Thanks, Pete. Maybe I'd
better have it. After all, I'm up here on business."

Nobody said a word. That whole procession just stood around and
waited. A bunch of ravens looking for the carcass. The game warden
pinned the badge back on his soggy pocket flap. He looked around at
that bunch of scissorbills and then at me. "Looks like the gang's all
here." He had a grin on his mug. "Think they might as well be in on
this?" "O.K. by me, Warden," I told him. "Nothin' hurts like the
truth."

Well, it's easier to suffer if you're comfortable. By the time we'd
all got set at the big table in the dining room, Velma and the Shoshone
gal had coffee poured for all hands. I didn't know hardly how to start
the ball a-rollin'. Tim Smithers' buck teeth was a-shinin' over between
the other two hunters so I could see that the stocks-and-bonds man
was going to enjoy this here kangaroo court. More than I was, by a
dern sight.

"Some of you fellers have heard what the game warden had to say,
and some of you haven't. So, to put my head in the lion's mouth, I'll
put you straight on whole deal. A hunter," (I had to gargle on that
one) "beefed to our warden that I run him off the place, after takin'
his earnest money. And that our food and service is horrible. Besides,
his cabin wasn't fit for a dog. *And*, Warren says, this gent claimed
that if my camp is run like my ranch is, my outfitter's license should
be taken away. *Also*, that I'm a crook. So you birds can see just who
you're 'sociatin' with."

"Haw, haw, haw!" Smithers couldn't hold it. "Doc, you and George here can see what us poor suckers are up against. Haw, haw, haw!" Being kind of jittery about this deal, I had my eye on Kompton. He seemed to look at Slim Wilson before he grinned around at Smithers. But the new horse wrangler was swirling his coffee around with a spoon and didn't seem to notice. Pete Elaby was seated in between Wilson and the game warden, and was smirking at me. He was having as much fun outa this meeting as the broker. Velma don't drink coffee, but she was standing in the doorway over by the kitchen watching. Sally wasn't in sight.

Well, I started out by telling how I started getting letters a long time before hunting season started from this gent in Kansas. "This Long inquired about rates I charged for huntin' big game. How far from ranch t' camp. Kind of tents." I had to think of the other sappy things he asked. "Oh, yeah, he wanted t' know did I have a good chef." I could hear Smithers snort at this. I could see the grins on Pete and Warren Kompton, who were well acquainted with old Shorty. I went on, "Did I have guides that knew their business and their places! Also did I have electric lights and heaters in camp. Was our water pure, and how about sanitation. He wanted to know if he shot some game he didn't want, could he exchange it?"

Nobody said a word for a while. Then Pete Elaby spoke up. "This jackass musta thought there ain't any more ethics in huntin' big game than there is in raisin' wheat an' storin' it for a subsidy." Oh, yes, I'd mentioned that he'd said several times he was the biggest wheat farmer in Kansas. Said he also had a big subsidy deal. Stored grain, too.

"Haw, haw, that smart damn sucker." Smithers was enjoying this.

"But when I wrote him that I required earnest money as a deposit, to book him as a sure hunter—that I could handle only a few, and that I could only run my business on reservations—well, he sent only part of the deposit."

The game warden had been listening intently to all this. Suddenly he said, "Bill, when you run him off, how about that deposit?" "You know, Warren," I found a paper I'd copied out of my account book, and handed it to him, "after th' ruckus I happened t' think of that. From our ranch rates for board an' cabin use, this geezer owes me around eight bucks."

I could see everybody smiling now, even the new horse wrangler. But the only one with a word to say was the broker. He says, "Haw, haw. That smart damn sucker. George, you and I, and Doc, here, we know how to get around ol' Bill now. Haw, haw!"

Kompton handed the paper back, but he still looked puzzled. "Warren, if you want ta look," I told him, "I still got all th' dern letters he sent." "Nope, Bill, the only thing left I'd like t'know," he was feeling better now, "why did you throw him and his hunting equipment off the place?

Little Sally was nowhere in sight, but Velma came out of the kitchen and got into it. "Bill, Sally finally told me all about it." Vel had a lopsided smile, but I could see she was still riled. "Day before yesterday, when she was serving Long the ham and eggs he asked for, Sally saw him pouring whisky into his coffee." She looked around the table with a grim smile. "When Sally put the tray down, that dumb ox threw his arm around her and pinched her. Then she slapped him as hard as she could. She said he shoved his chair back, stood up and roared, 'take that back and bring me something fit to eat! I don't like foreigners to handle my food anyhow!' " Velma started to swell up and get peeved then. "I heard what he said from the kitchen. Then the front door slammed and I saw him stomp past the kitchen windows towards his cabin."

Pete spoke up, "By hell, when Velma come down t' th' corral t' get Bill on th' job, I wouldn't got in that lady's way f'r seven hunderd dollars."

You'da thought this was a play the women's club down at Roaring River puts on in the winter time, the way this bunch was acting. Even forgot their coffee.

"Yeah," I told them, "when I got up ta where he was, I was about ta crown him where his little horns sprout, but Velma punched me in th' ribs. So I made him apologize ta Sally. Thought he'd pull out then, but he stuck around anyhow."

The game warden still wasn't satisfied. "You didn't throw him off, then?" By the time I told Warren about the visit in Long's cabin next morning, how th' wheat baron had built me up, and then the proposition to go bring in a bull elk and a buck deer for him, the game warden was mad. Velma said, "Just then, you know, Bill, there was a phone call for you that morning. I sent Sally over to Long's cabin to get you. You'd left the door open a bit. She got there just in time to hear Long's proposition. When you started throwing things, you just missed her with that first big gun case. I got there just as you hung that portable toilet around his neck."

Everybody was hee-hawing at Velma by this time. I thought Elaby's jacks must be there. Then she said, "I brought my rolling pin to help out, but when I got there I thought I'd have to use it on you to protect the man from Kansas."

20

"Haw, haw, haw, Bill, you poor damn sucker!" Smithers' teeth made me think of an alligator I seen in a circus one time.

It was about time to hit the sack, so I stood up and said, "I reckon that's about it, Warren. Th' show's over. If you wanta give my outfitter's license to th' man from Kansas, you're welcome."

That game warden had a big smile on his face when he rubbed at the bear's grease we'd put on his singed brisket. He stood up and put out his hand. "Bill, you're all there. I'm going down to Roaring River and see about some business.'" He wouldn't stay all night, said he had to go down to see about storing some wheat. He shook hands all around, wished us all luck, and left.

Chapter Three

Pete and I made sure the three hunters were comfortable for the night in the big cabin they were sharing. As we walked toward the ranch cabin, Pete stopped off at the bunkhouse. The tall wrangler had the gas lamp lit and was unrolling his bed. I was about to bid them goodnight when something itched me up above. "Pretty snug camp you guys got here," I looked at the pinups Tony Belknap, last year's wrangler, had stuck around on the log walls. They both laughed. "Plumb domestic," Elaby said, looking at Wilson. Slim had his boots off and was laying his socks across the tops. "Sure homey to have our girl friends' pictures around." I turned to go out the door, past Wilson's saddle with his blanket and chaps draped over it. "Oh, Slim, just happened to think. Did you know Warren Kompton? Had an idea you were old friends." As he gave me a quick glance, I saw Pete, hanging up his hat and jacket, watching Wilson. "You know, Bill, when I got a ride up to Roaring River with th' mail driver, I asked him if he knew anybody that could use a horse wrangler." He looked over at his saddle, then at Elaby and I. "He told me th' game warden would probably know. When I finally found him and we'd jawed awhile, Kompton said he didn't know, offhand. Said he'd keep an eye out." Slim looked at Pete and grinned. "If I hadn't needed a haircut, I'd a missed a payin' job, and a good show throwed in free."

The next morning after breakfast we were on the trail to camp. We left the ranch in good hands. I figured Velma and Sally could take care of most anything that came up. Pete Elaby would be at the ranch to take care of the wrangling and maintenance. He would pack supplies and gear out to the camp, and pack hunters, trophies, game meat and gear back to the ranch. " 'Pay Load Elaby,' that's what they call me, Bill." Pete had a homestead a few miles below Roaring River. With us four pack mules, saddle horse, and the bell mare, he made a good living in the life he loved. He'd packed for the Forest Service all spring and summer, and made a deal with me to do most of my packing, and was going to winter with us at the ranch. It wasn't far, only about eight miles, to camp. When we got there, Shorty Beel was cleaning up the cook tent and Buck Bruen was sawing wood. AND, dang my britches if MISTER Austen Hackett wasn't splitting and stacking it! In at the ranch, he was about the fussiest, most fidgity, "dang git on with the show," kind of geezer I ever saw. As Buck was going to guide him and Shorty was going to do the feeding, I was getting out of the maybe agony I figgered the guide and cook would have to go through.

For some reason, Hackett was a changed man. Now, he was the picture of a genial, hail-fellow-well-met, I-love-everybody kind of bird. This corporation lawyer said he'd had the time of his life; and that after ten days in camp with Shorty and Buck, he had an education, with a degree that he had, for *once*, really earned. And that now he was *blood brothers* with Bruen and Beel.

I noticed that he had a bad limp with his left leg, and was going to ask him how come, when my sweaty saddle horse started to roll. I forgot about it till afterwards.

When I asked him what kinda luck he'd had hunting, he sorta flushed up and said, "Well, you know, I passed up several shots at elk. Good ones. Missed several times." The lawyer gave me a grim smile. "You'll have to ask Buck about that. I'm going to take a big doe deer back home, though. Saw some bear, but passed "em up. Best trip of my life."

In the middle of the flurry of getting the three hunters settled in their tent, and helping the boys unpack the camp supplies and the hunters' gear, Al Neeman rode into camp. "Got to the ranch a couple hours after you'd all pulled out. Brought th' mail from Roaring River." Al got around to shaking hands with everybody. Just as Pete Elaby, with Mr. Hackett's deer and possessions loaded on his jacks, was starting back up the trail to the ranch, Al hollered, "Hold up, Pete. Here's a couple letters for Mr. Hackett."

Hackett on his horse, following Pete's big sorrel, pulled up and rode over to where I was standing by the corral. He leaned over, put his hand on my shoulder, and said, "Bill, those two blood brothers of mine over there took the *Mister* off my name, and now I'm 'Old Give-and-Take Hackett,' if any body should ask you." Hackett straightened in his saddle and took a long look back up the Buffalo Fork and around up to Terrace Mountain. "I'm coming back next year, Bill, if you'll put me in camp with my old professors, Buck and Shorty." *That*, coming from Hackett, made me sure he'd rolled in *somethin'* holy.

He shook hands again, hollered, "So long, everybody," and trotted his horse around the fringe of timber to catch up with Pete and his pack string.

After supper, when the three hunters had gone to their tent, I found

Hackett was a changed man.

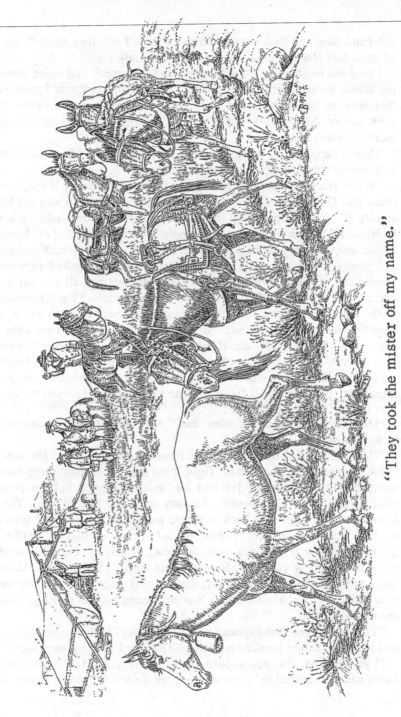

"They took the mister off my name."

out from Beel and Bruen about some of that "I dub thee knight" kind of gush that Hackett used, and about his gimpy leg.

I told the boys about poor Vincent and his arrest, and some about the wheat baron's hard luck. Looking around the cook tent I realized that now we had a full crew: cook, horse wrangler, and a guide for each hunter. Maybe this was going to be a good hunt without any more shenanigans.

Then I happened to remember about Hackett's stiff leg. So Buck and Shorty started to give us the deadwood.

"When Hackett shot, that sure ruined a good sneak we'd made on them elk. Good bull in th' bunch, too." Buck lit a match and got his smelly ol' pipe a-goin'. "That thick-headed sap was sure riled up when he heard th' branch-breakin' an' thumpin' when that band of elk bored a hole inta tha heavy timber. All we got outa th' deal was fresh manure an' plenty of tracks. All I could do was cuss," he sucked in some smoke and grinned, "when I looked past Hackett and all I could see was a mess of black feathers at the foot of a big fir tree." Buck frowned at the memory. "Seems like five or six big ravens had been havin' a hard time lately. You could see some of 'em on a high branch a-waitin'. They musta been arguin' about th' next move f'r a full belly. I figger they seen th' elk; then they seen us make our sneak. They wasn't born yesterday. They knew what we was up to. One of th' boss ravens got impatient about waitin', I figger. So he flew dow ta see what th' hell was holdin' up the' grub pile."

"Didja ever see them elk after that?" Wilson had listened intently to Buck's story.

"Hell, no, Slim," Buck shook his head at the memory of Hackett. "That lawyer had me half on th' fight 'bout then. Had spent three-four hours making *that* sneak. Hackett had missed a good bull an hour after we left camp that mornin'. An easy shot. 'So,' I told him, 'This fixes that bunch. Let's git back ta where we tied up our horses.' When we left, I could hear them ravens still a-flutterin' around an' waitin' for their pardner ta fly back with the news. Well, we angled around them parks below Nowlin Mountain and down Line Creek. Heard some bulls buglin' up high, about dark. It was plumb black when we rode inta camp, an' Hackett hadn't even opened his yap since he shot the raven."

"You remember that saphead from Kentucky?" Al Neeman really had a trigger happy hunter last year. "The one I give up on, Buck?"

"I sure do, Al. But you shoulda had this Hackett. Hell's bells. He damn near stampeded th' pack string after we left th' ranch, when he just *had* t' shoot a porkypine. I wasn't watchin' him that time. Bill, you remember that fat ol' rockchuck that's been thumbin' his nose an givin' us that monkeyface grin all these years on that rocky point about North Fork? Yep, Ol' Trigger-happy had t' blast him, too."

Shorty started filling our coffee cups and making a lot of racket filling the stove with wood. Al and Slim Wilson hadn't said a word for quite a while, but I could see Shorty was wrinkling up that seamy old mug to get in his half on Hackett. But Shorty didn't get his chance, because Buck Bruen was puffing that smoke like Casey Jones, and had just got warmed up.

"When me an' ol' Shorty was unpackin' the horses to set up camp, this gent blows a hole, big as a washtub, in a fat ol' snowshoe rabbit. Throwed blood 'n' guts all over his own fine eiderdown sleeping bag, a-layin' over by some panniers." Buck jerked his thumb at the grinning cook. "You oughta seen th' way Shorty watched him when he put th' grub on th' table. A few nights ago Hackett told us he's a-goin' t' make a *sportsman* outa his boy when he gits big enought t' handle a *gun*! Yessirree, he says, th' great outdoors and these here mountains is just th' place f'r a *he-man*."

"Yeah, he-man." Shorty had his sourdough keg on the table and was pouring a little potato water in it. "One mornin', while Buck was wranglin' horses, old Lead Spazzum was tryin' ta kill my chipmunks with that dang gold inlaid .22 that he'd had special made. What I told that gink wouldn't work out in Sunday School. I figgered mebbe he'd soon be outa shells. An' from what Buck an' I seen, his big gun was goin' ta go hungry. I keep mine hid, an' Buck's ought-six ain't his caliber." The cook stirred the sourdough with a long-handled spoon, and then started to wrap a blanket around the keg, but he wasn't through yet. "Say, you birds shoulda heard ol' Buck give 'im a talk about live and let live. Supprized me all ta hell. Didn't think Buck had it in him. Killin' them chipmunks got Buck's dander up, too."

Bruen, shaving a pitchy stick for morning fire lighter, was grinning at Shorty's cackling. "Yeah, when Buck give Hackett a lecture 'bout tit-f'r-tat an' survival of the fittest an' nachur's laws, you birds shoulda seen th' silly grin that lawyer give ol' Buck. I thought Buck was gonna blow th' plug when Hackett tells 'im, 'Who'd ever think you'd find a Holy Roller preacher out in these mountains?'"

When the cook took out his uppers and started to whittle on the plastic with a hunting knife, we leaned over to watch the operation. Suddenly Shorty waved the teeth in the air and dang near hit th' stovepipe. "Buck got red around th' gills at Hackett's crack, but he told th' hunter, 'sometimes th' cure is tougher'n th' disease, Mr. Hackett. Mebbe Mother Nature'll even up in th' long run."

Slim Wilson had been watching the cook and the guide with more'n ordinary attention. Suddenly he punched Al Neeman in the ribs and slid his coffee cup over the rough board table. "Bill, you're nearest th' pot. An', while you're pourin', let me ask you an' Al here: did you ever see a cook an' a guide who could *ever* afford gold inlaid handles on their hunting knives? And look at them scabbards hangin' on their wore-out ol' belts! Hand carved an' fancy as hell!"

Beel and the guide leered at each other and Shorty snickered, "Let Buck tell yuh what happened that mornin'. Boy, I'd like ta seen that." I reached over on the Rema stove to get the big pot of coffee, and poured everybody a mug. The cook stuffed wood in the firebox, and tied the tent flaps down. The wrangle horse, Wilson had tied on a picket log out in the park back of camp, started to nicker. Wilson uncoiled his long length out from under the table, and untied the flaps.

Buck had just got started when Slim got back from his look-see in the dark. "Horse is O.K. Just lonesome."

Buck said he had wrangled late that morning, and as the horse wrangler sat down again, the old guide was saying: " 'Bout sunup that mornin', Hackett and I was on our horses an' leavin'. Snowin' a little when we left camp, an' th' white stuff changed th' look of th' landscape.

"I sure got a bang outa ol' Lead Slinger that mornin'." Buck was grinning kinda sly. "While we was ridin' up th' trail I could hear ol' Shorty, choppin' wood back at th' tents. So cold that it sounded as if he was slicin' steel with a sledge hammer." Bruen had that old mountain man smirk, when he said, "I looked back at Hackett, ridin' along behind me. He seemed kinda spooky at th' way th' weather had changed. Them rims an' ridges south of the Buffalo looked like dim, frosty, now-or-never ghosts from the Arctic. Th' timbered benches an' terraces on Terrace Mountain woulda sent a polar bear high-tailin' ta Florida, it was that frosty. Jest a sifty needle a frost a-fallin'. I'll bet Hackett," Buck gave an imitation of a he-man snicker, "wondered if them game magazines had told th' truth about huntin' in the' Rockies, haw, haw. . . . Well," he went on, opening up his shirt front, "Shorty, you sure banked this cook tent tight. That fire'll run us outa here."

Al shoved his shoulder against me and says, "Git over by th' tent flap, Bill. We ain't a-goin' ta let them hit the bed roll till these knife stealers tell th' truth. You gittin' sleepy, Slim?" Wilson shoved his

28

coffee mug over again. "I'm just gettin' woke up," and he squinted at me. "We got to get t' th' bottom of this," I told Bruen. "That was sure some limp Hackett had, Buck."

The guide started fumbling for his tobacco sack. "Well, them ponies we was ridin' sure had rollers up their noses. They was shivery an' hated ta face inta them icicle snowflakes. After we had climbed above South Fork Falls, they got warmed up an' knew they was in for it. That trail is shore steep." He paused to light that smelly old thing. "A coupla miles below Pendergraf meadows, I heard some bull elk a-talkin' on them timbered slopes up north of the trail. Boy, on these frosty winter's-comin' mornin's them old bulls bugle their heads off. You'd think from the music they was puttin' out, that Nowlin Mountain was their last stand.

"Well, I turned Baldy up th' mountain. You fellers know that trail that finally zigzags up 'n' over, then down ta Crater Lake? One thing I gotta hand Hackett, he always kept up and didn't lag behind, like lotsa hunters do. I noticed he had his eye on me, and the way he handled that black horse mebbe meant he wasn't foolin'. We should be dressin' out a good bull pretty soon. Mebbe his trigger finger is numb, I hoped. The closer we got to them grassy benches and long narrow parks, the more bulls we could hear. We was a mile or two above the old Angle camp just up from th' White Canyon. The climb up that steep timber-covered mountain had our nags winded, so we stopped for a breather.

"You know, durin' all this time that hunter hadn't said a word. Mebbe too cold." Bruen tamped more weed into his pipe. "Well, the snow had let up a little. I wet my finger ta git th' wind, an' listened ta several bull elk. Most of 'em seemed ta be in these pot holes and benches below an' west of us. Them ol' stinkers was callin' each other bad names and darin' th' cowards. Sittin' on Ol' Baldy a-rubbin' his sweaty nose on a knee, I sneaked a look at th' Lead Slinger. He was kinda jitterin' in th' saddle an' nervous as all hell. But Blacky didn't give a damn. He looked like he was tired of us damn hunters anyhow . . . Say, you fellers gittin' tired of me an' Hackett?" We all told Buck to keep a-goin'. "Well, I made sign for him ta git off his pony. I got off mine, and took my '06 out of the scabbard. Then I tied both horses ta trees close ta th' trail, at the edge of a narrow park. Snow was three, four inches deep, and that high, snowy ridge between us and Sody Fork looked like friz crocodile teeth, up on end. All the heavy timber was ice frosted. Looked like Christmas with the Arctic D.T.s. Hack didn't look happy but he was game.

"Finally, seein' Hackett had his blunderbuss an' was set ta go, I whispered to him about how we was goin' ta pussyfoot west along this timber-fringed bench. There was a lusty bull soundin' off close by, just below in th' heavy pines. Hackett whispered, 'Buck, I'll do just what you say, this is for real.' Well, I figgered, we'll soon have this over with. So I took off, crunching along easy-like, stoppin' now an' then ta listen. Hack was watchin' close, followin' along O.K. Stoppin' - startin' - listen' - makin' sign ta Hackett - him noddin' - wind O.K. - bull below us - not movin' - gittin' louder - hear rivals blowin' off - gittin' close.

"Well, we went 200 yards, mebbe more, up - down - pockets - sink holes - alkali licks - blowdowns - deadfall jungle - then fine open timber - wind change a little - Hackett O.K. - followin' good. Well, I stopped, held up my hand. There, just below us - mebbe 60 yards - I could see a helluva good 6-point bull. We was behind trees. He was just below us - plain sight - buttin' an' slashin' small scrubby trees, an' gruntin'. Could see plain glimpses of fat cow elk slowly browsin' on th' snowy grass an' bushes. Those shadowy forms helped their blusterin' boss show up good. I looked around ta see if Hack was on th' job, cause there was his bull. Yessirree, I mighta knowed it. I looked around just in time ta see Old Killer throw up his highclass gun and *gut shoot* a big mule deer doe! She was jest about a throw rope's length away.

"While my yap was bouncin' around on my briskit, he snapped another shot, which missed, at her floppy eared fawn. It jest stood there, big wonder in its eyes, lookin' down at its dyin' maw, moanin' an' kickin' th' blood-soaked snow around.

"When that bull and his harem tore off down that jungled-up spruce mountain side, them thuds an' that limb-breakin' clatter woke up even that gut-shootin' jackass hunter.

"By hell, Bill, I done forgot my grandad was a hard-shell Baptist; or mebbe it come back ta me. I musta warmed up them frosty pines we was under, 'cause I got ta drippin' sweat. I told that Hackett bird just what a low, mother-murderin', two-bit, infantile, underhanded, gunpowder delinquent I thought he was. I sorta plain insinuated that he musta conceived himself, that no mortal man or woman coulda had any part of manufacturin' any such so-called two-legged human. That no animal I'd never seen would ever be caught associatin' with his lonely unethical carcass.

"I musta put over these playful remarks to this lawyer cause he didn't have no—what's the word?—no rebuttal! I admitted, though I

30

dang near didn't, that the game laws for this area allowed the hunting of deer of both sexes. It was legal, but even most human ghouls let the kids have their mothers awhile.

"Old Trigger Happy had set down on a log about then. He couldn't bear to look at that graceful fawn, she was a-hidin' close by in a stand of spruce, watchin' me clean the innards out of her maw. I couldn't hardly stand that, either. I cleaned my knife on the rotten tree he was a-settin' on. Real nasty, I was. A guide's got ta make a livin', an' most of us *are* meat eaters, but sometimes some people have a way of making a guide's life plumb shameful, I told him. Mebbe I was mean, but I was mad, damn mad!

"While Hackett was a-settin' there on that rotten deadfall lookin' at his imported gunbarrel he sorta looked homesick, and dammed if I didn't feel plumb ashamed of my damfool jabber. But thinkin' back, dammed if I didn't backslide again.

"I told him, 'Now, Hackett,' (no Mister, I'm a-tellin' you), I says, 'Hackett, I'm a-goin back t'git th' horses, so's we can take your deer back t' camp. If I find you gone when I git back in a half hour or so, you'll have t' *walk* back t' camp, and I don't mean *mebbe*!'

"Well, fellas, I grabbed my rifle and took off in th' direction of where we'd tied our horses. I figgered Hackett could build a fire (he had matches) to warm up his cold carcasss and dumb cranium. When I got to th' horses and was ridin' along leading his black, I figgered I'd put th' deer on Baldy an' I'd walk back t' camp. *That* hunter couldn'ta made it himself.

"Well, when I got back t' th' deer, that damfool Hackett wasn't there. Back when I was dressin' out th' deer it started t' snow. Now they was big flakes, big as a half dollar - fallin' fast - really comin' down. I tied up them nags, close by th' deer, made big circles around, huntin' sign. Snow'd even covered them runaway elk tracks. Finally I fired some signal shots - waited - snowin' like hell - fired some more - no answer - waited. Wind comin' up - snowin' hard - fired some more shots - waited - thought I faintly heard a shot - plumb faint - mebbe. Couldn't tell direction. Couldn't hardly see th' horses tied t' th' trees. Shot again. Well - I got ta lookin' in my coat pockets, then in my chaps pockets. Hell's bells - only got two shells left. Why, hell. I went over ta th' horses and felt around in Hackett's saddle-bag. He had two boxes - damnit - wouldn't fit mine - wrong caliber. Snowin' harder now. Dark that high up among the snow clouds - dark and cold.

"Well, I dunno what *you* birds woulda done. But here's what *I* done. I cut a lotta green branches with lots of needles. Balsam, I reckon. Put th' doe carcass, hair up, on some dead branches, then covered that warm meat with them green branches, I got that done. Oh, yeah I hollered quite a few times, figgerin' Hackett might be near or comin'. Didn't wanta shoot my last two shells. Heard nothin'. Hollered some more. Nope, nothin' but th' drivin' snow in that black timber. Naw, Bill, no echo, storm too low up in them timbered benches. Finally I could barely see, so I got them paper sack lunches Shorty give us. Put 'em in that old coat I keep tied behind my cantle. Wrote that dumb lawyer a note, and pegged it to a big tree trunk right next to Hack's doe. Hung the coat over it. then I got on Baldy an' led th' black. Got back down to Shorty an' th' cook tent 'bout midnight."

"Yeah, later'n that, Buck." Beel had followed every word. "Remember when you told me what happened? I ast why didn't you leave Blackie tied up so's Hackett could ride him t' camp if he come back t' th' deer. Buck told me that Hackett would probably git in more trouble than he was, if he'd left Blackie. Blackie'd come back t' camp if he had his head, but knowin' how Hackett is, he'd try t' guide th' horse, an' he'd end up on Buffalo Plateau or Blackie'd buck him off and come home alone. Anyhow, that's th' way it was."

" 'Anyhow, that's the way it was,' says you." I got kind of ringy then at Buck. Slim Wilson and Al Neeman stared at Buck and Shorty, then at me. "That's the way it was, *hell*! We're not goin' ta let two baby-snatchin' knife-stealers quit there, are we, boys?" Wilson and Al held their coffee cups over, and Shorty, grinning, filled them up. While Buck hammered out and refilled his briar, Shorty reached into some rawhide panniers and came out with a big pan full of raisin cookies. He set them down in the middle of the table, and then rushed around to the pile of wood behind the stove. He pushed Al out of the way to grab a stick, and rushed back to the panniers, mumbling, "Give 'em an inch an' they'll take a mile." Two big fat chipmunks appeared on the table top, running for their lives. When one fell in the pan of cookies, Buck got excited, dropped his pipe in his coffee mug, and started to shake the pan.

While everybody was laughin' and kiddin' the zoo-keepin' cook, Slim got the cook's dishrag, and was mopping up the coffee. By the time Bruen had his washed-out pipe a-goin', and all had started on the cookies, we got Buck goin' again on how Hackett got baptized into mountain religion.

"Neither Shorty or I slept much that night." Buck started to rub at his eyes and it must have been catching. All of us started to yawn, but he was too close to the end to sleep now. Buck went on: "Well, we'll have t' tell it like Hackett told us. We wasn't there. Here's about how it went."

After Buck took off at a fast walk in the direction of the horses, he left the hunter to build a fire to warm up his chilling body and mixed frame of mind. He got it started after awhile, with bunches of dead needles, and squaw wood from the tree trunks. He turned round and round to warm up by it. He sat and squirmed kinda uncomfortable on his log. Hack finally admitted to himself that Buck's vociferous comments held a lot of honest truth. He churned over and over all the incidents of the hunt up to now. He saw what a figure he would cut, after all his brags, if he came back without a big bull elk. It started to snow harder, the hunter heard some trotting thumps halt in the open timber below him. Staring with unbelief, he saw a big antlered bull elk smelling and pawing with angry grunts at the tracks and sign of the recently departed band of elk. Slowly he raised his gun. As he was about to lower the boom on his trophy, the uneasy bull gave a whirling lunge, and swiftly faded into the jungle of dark timber below. The silent disappearance of his wildly revived hopes quickly erased the guide's instructions. Hackett jumped up and trotted off down the hill, right on the bull's plain tracks. The snow started falling again, right after a lull in the wind, but his new sign was plain to see and follow over the older tracks left by the other elk.

In about an hour, after a lot of false starts, stops, and hard tumbles over the now-slick down timber, and jumbles of brushy roots, the breathless hunter, heart thumping, saw close by a bull elk staring at him with an astounded air of "What in hell is this kind of animal?" The bull let the hunter get his trembling gun up. As he aimed, and started to pull the trigger, he slipped on a slanted wet branch and fell wildly, with the gun exploding, and a numbed feeling in his shaky left leg. When he slowly got up, he didn't look for the elk. He stared with frightened eyes at his bloody wool pants, and felt the burning shock of his wound. With shaking hands, Austen Hackett unbuckled his heavy pants. Exploring fearfully, he found the deep crease of a painful flesh wound, just above the kneecap.

He tore off strips of his underwear and wrapped them tightly around the shredded skin and the bloody groove. He painfully flexed his leg. It still worked. Thanking his Maker, he finally was able to stand up stiffly, and saw that he could still navigate. He brushed the wet soggy pine needles and clinging black dirt from his weak and shivering body, and looked around for his cherished rifle. The bolt and bore were chuck full of sandy dirt and snowy twigs and needles, as the gun had skidded under some fallen dead branches. It had stuck, butt up and barrel down, dug into the wet black earth of a pocket gopher's hill.

He cleaned off his gun, and blew and scraped the bore clean. Then he found he had just one live shell left to his terrified lonely name. His extra boxes of ammunition he'd left in the small saddle bag on his hunting horse. He groaned at the thicker falling big flakes, and hobbled in an aimless, painful circle. And now he remembered old Buck's final warning. He tried frantically to figure the direction up the steep, slippery mountain, back to the dead doe.

About that time, he heard three carefully spaced signal shots. As he slowly raised his gun to fire in answer, he heard another three shots. He pulled the trigger, and got only a dull click. As he pulled back the bolt to reason why, he heard a third salvo. Seeing nothing wrong with the firing pin, he shoved home the bolt, pulled the trigger, and felt only a dull ping. He had a dud, a dead shell. Listening, he heard three final shots.

The lost hunter tried to locate the direction of the signals, aware that the snow, now falling heavily, the rising wind, and the prison walls of thick timber were defeating his desperately straining ears. Listen as he would, he could hear no more shots. As he started up in the direction he hoped was right, he figured that the lunch he had tied on his saddle was worth a hundred bucks. He was lost and hurt, and his belly was empty. Finally, he thought of his own tracks—he could follow them back to the deer's carcass. Crestfallen, he found no sign, the falling snow had hidden them all. Anyway, it had to be up. Back and forth, painfully up and up, he hobbled. He found himself using his beloved rifle as a crutch. The cold, dismal darkness slipped up on the agony of his climbing and falling journey. He stopped weakly under a mass of dead trees, hung up slantwise in the crotch of an enormous green spuce's receiving arms. Just as the black snowy night fell, the crippled-up hunter finally got a fire going in the shelter nature had so conveniently provided.

Hackett's leg was bleeding slightly, and the makeshift bandage was clotted up. He managed to wash off the painful gouge with fresh snow, and ripped up the rest of his undershirt to fix up fresh bandaging. Now he felt some better; but the leg throbbed with pain, and had stiffened up.

That night was forever etched in Hackett's memory, he said. The sequence of fitful snatches of sleep, mixed with self-recrimination and anger at the fix he was in, putting branches on the sheltering fire,

34

and shaking gobs of wet snow from his tired body, made a weary nightmare. Finally there was light seeping through his branchy roof. He was thankfully aware that he was still alive. His heavy wool pants and good hunting coat had protected him, his mountain retreat was fairly dry, and he had a sort of bed of piled-up dead branches, and pine boughs he'd hacked off with his hunting knife. Standing up and hobbling around was a harsh experience, but he felt no throbbing in his leg, and was much relieved.

About then, he heard a commotion of whirring wings and weird gobbling calls. In the clearing sky above him he saw a string of ravens, and he caught a glimpse of other birds, flying in a straight line, just about the height of the surrounding timber. He felt a wild jolt of revived hope. Shivering with excitement, he remembered some of Buck's remarks: something acid about city people with no more sense that to mistreat animals and birds that could really help them.

Old Trigger-Happy suddenly grabbed his three-hundred-dollar, walnut-butted crutch. Digging its blue barrel into the crusted snow, he took off on the black guides' raucous trail. He had to pause for agonized intervals of heartpounding, sweating gulps of air and rest, all the while wildly straining his ears. The noise was gradually receding over the tall timber tops. He climbed and staggered for nearly half a mile, seemed like a hundred. His leg-and-a-half gait was hampered by boggy swamps, willow clumps, blow-downs, and deadfalls. Now the miserable man came close to a jumbled-up noise of squalling, chattering, and calling.

He came out on a very small park, to view a couple of dozen or so of assorted sizes of ravens, camp-robbers, and Clark's crows, flying, dodging, in a frenzy of cleaning up the forest. Old Step-and-a-half had seen this spot before. The twitters, screams, and hoarse calls made the most welcome music he'd ever heard. Busy birds were flying about with scraps of bloody meat and entrails, perched on branches, chewing, pecking, scolding, and fighting for more food. Two or three enormous black members of the Sanitary Division had started to pull away the green pine branches off the deer's carcass. They had cleaned up the remains of the paunch, they were now going to uncover and work on the main course. This made up the most heartwarming picture old Trigger-Happy had ever seen.

His rescuers seemed to resent his blowsy presence. They were all busy at the serious business of making a living, so they gave him an angry cussing in their various squally voices. When he hobbled closer, to enjoy the location, they all flew up and perched in snowy treetops

He took off on the black guides' raucous trail.

and on various limbs and branches, there to stare with angry eyes at his bedraggled form. After the peculiar salutations and ceremonies of this welcoming committee of the cleanup squad had subsided into sudden squawks and muttered squally remarks, the limpy hunter took a better look around. There was an old shabby coat hanging from a snaggy limb on a near-by tree. When he hobbled over and took hold of it, he saw a piece of lunch-sack paper pegged on the rough spruce bark sheltered by it. Printed in heavy pencil was the message:

TRIGGER HAPPY—IF YOU GIT BACK HERE—*STAY PUT*— WE'LL COME BACK HERE—YOUR LUNCH IN COAT POCK- ET—P.S. *STAY PUT—YOU SAP*

As his shaking hands fumbled the lunch in its heavy paper sack out of the pocket, Mr. Hackett thought, "Why, that's the best love letter I ever read." And as he ravenously ate the tasty frozen sandwiches, grabbing up handfuls of snow to wash the food down, he thought, "Boy, can Shorty cook good grub!"

The storm had let up, now and then the sun came out, but the weather on that snow-covered mountain was still cold. When he had just about licked up all the crumbs and felt better, a great blob of wet snow fell off a straining branch, and he was the unwilling target. After he had brushed and shaken off this wet embrace, he got the shivers. He struggled with wet wood awhile, and finally got a fire going.

Suddenly the black clad members of the Sanitary Division flew up in excitement, and off over the timber tops on silent wings. Trigger- Happy looked around in fright, but he could see no reason for the alarm. The other birds paid no attention, continuing to chatter and whistle, flying down now and then as close as they dared, to snatch and grab at the visible scraps.

In a few minutes, even the hunter could hear the thumping, cloddy noise of approaching animals. Buck Bruen rode up, leading a pack horse. Close behind rode Shorty Beel, leading a saddle horse. Just about then, here came the giant crows, flying back to perch on tree tops and branches, muttering dark comments and watching with their cunning black peepers.

"Well, when ol' Shorty an' me rode up there that mornin'," Bruen shook his head, "yuh wouldn'ta believed it. I still don't."

Beel started to cackle in his squeaky voice. "Hackett was a-settin' on a big dead log kinda nursin' a smoky fire. It was blowin' right in his face. He was th' raggedest, dirtiest, ol' throwed-out lawyer I ever seen." Shorty watched as Buck started t' ream out his pipe with that gold-handled knife. "Yeah, danged if he didn't look glad t' see us.

He kinda staggered around when he stood up. He says somethin' t' Buck about gittin' a love letter Buck had left on a tree, somethin' about framin' the best love letter he ever got, t' keep on his desk." Buck swung at him. Beel leered, and finished, "I didn't know Buck could write love letters."

"Yeah, and that cook," Buck dug an affectionate thumb into Shorty's thin ribs. "When Hackett looked like he was goin' t' kiss Shorty, you shoulda seen him duck, an' lose his uppers in th' snow.

"When he started ta walk over ta us, I seen him stagger; he was talkin' kinda silly-like about my sandwiches. I see he's weaker'n a cat." Shorty looked at the new shoe-packs he was wearing. Kinda self-conscious, I thought.

Buck had his eyes squinted, thinking back. "While Shorty untied a sack of grub from behind his cantle, I tied our four horses t' trees close t' th' doe's carcass.

"We go ta lookin' over Hackett's leg, when he told us what happened," Shorty said. "He didn't wanta show us. But we built up a big fire, melted snow, an' made coffee in a big can I packed along. While he was gittin' stoked up, me an' Buck cut th' seam on his pants an' looked at his shot-up leg. Jest a shreddy kind of crease, clean, too. Didn't look bad. I took my bottle of iodine, I keep for wood ticks, and sloshed it good. Man, that lead slinger was lucky, Buck figgered we'd put salt poultices on it at camp."

Buck started to laugh. "Shorty, you remember when you sloshed that big bottle of iodine on him, an' he hollered?" The cook grunted, "Yeah, them big ravens, waitin' their turn, croakin' again. Damn things thought he was cheatin' 'em outa a good meal."

I knew Buck wanted to get this story over, he was yawning again.

"Shorty untied th' pack horse, and I started t' pull th' green branches, what them ravens hadn't, off th' doe. Th' cook was startin' t' tighten th' cinches an' I had just got th' sling rope fixed when Beel grabbed at my coat 'n' jerked his head. We looked over at the hunter. He'd just burned up the lunch wrappin's an' was tryin' t' hobble over to us. He'd start t'talk, then kinda gargle, 'n' git red in th' face. He sorta had us two birds worried, I'll tell yuh. Then, when we grabbed a-holt of the deer ta throw it across th' pack horse, Hack held up both hands, his wet mittens a-steamin' in th' cold. He said, kinda mixed-up an' choky, 'Wait a minute, fellas. Now this is hard t' say, but it's gonna be done.' That dirty mug, whickers, muddy kinda squint in his eye, looked sorta looney. He'd look up at them ravens, sittin' on their limbs, then further off at them others, waitin'. Then Hack would look

38

He said, "Wait a minute, fellers."

down at th' deer carcass, kinda limp an' hopeless it looked. I was gittin' spooked about then. I leaned up against Sleepy, that bay pack-horse, and looked over at th' cook, ta se if he was seein' what I was.

"Ol' Shorty let go th' deer's leg, and scratchin' that empty gray noodle, was a-glarin' suspicious-like. He musta thought ol' Trigger-Happy was floatin' off, while we sorta stood around in a trance. An' then Hack said, 'Before you start that doe on her last journey, I've got t' say somethin','' an' he finally come out with somethin' Shorty an' I still don't believe. It was somethin' like "Boys, the teeter-totter of nature had me balanced on th' light end. Last night I saw that, to survive, I'd better get my big feet on *both* sides of th' middle. This morning proved that. I have lived in th' lonesome little world of *me and mine*.' By this time I figured I knew just who th' Holy Roller preacher was. This gent was really shook. Then he said, 'Now, if you'll let me into your friendly big world of *us and ours*, I'd appreciate th' favor.' Me an' Sleepy and Shorty was plumb petrified, but that's what th' man said! When we stepped over th' doe's carcass t' shake hands with Hackett, I looked up, and dang if one of them ravens didn't wink. When we shook hands, I says, 'Hack, you're 'nishiated inta our ancient an' honorable old club. We'll now call you Old-Give-and Take.' When us three members shook hands, them impatient members of th' Sanitary Division broke inta loud croakin' caws. Then they looked down at us with them smart beady eyes. I tell yuh old Hack was really shook!"

Well, now we got the lowdown on Hackett's limp, all hands settled down for a good night's sleep. We got an early start next morning, but by luck no one of our men connected. The hunters were all soft and not used to the altitude. By late afternoon, we were all back in camp. Shorty needed a spud hole dug in the back of the cook tent; he was afraid of a freeze-up; his spuds, onions, canned milk and tomatoes needed protection. So we cleared out some of this kitchen panniers and went to work. We soon had the hole dug, and the grub stored in it. Shorty got out some of his good doughnuts and coffee as a reward. While the cook carefully put some blankets over the stacked grub and boarded up the hole, Al Neeman and Doc Forrester told us about coming across the remains of two buck mule deer, which by the signs had locked horns and died on the battle ground. So the talk got around to the things that happen and could happen to the inhabitants of most any wilderness country.

"Reminds me o' findin' a horse skeleton up on a game trail one time. Was nothin' like what th' doctor and I saw today." Al took another sip of coffee and squinted back into his memory. "Huntin' elk by myself. Ridin' down this game trail on th' crest of a high ridge. Open timber on both sides. Head of Calf Creek, it was. Rode past a tree and then a hundred feet or so, recollected I saw somethin' outa th' corner of one eye, looked kinda strange. I turned my horse an' rode back. 'Bout five feet up th' trunk of this big lodgepole pine was an old rope, real old. Th' bark had grown over it, hid most of it but the end hangin' down. Was plumb rotten. I got off my pony for a better look. Th' rope crumbled up an' fell apart when I touched it. Got ta lookin' fer more story. Then I saw parts of a horse's skull, lower jaw in pieces, but the skull an' nose parts around. Grass grown all through it. Tied my horse to same tree, an' went down th' steep grassy timbered slope t' look. Kicked up an old rusty bit with small pieces of old leather hangin' on it. Some horse teeth. I kicked around some more. Found a buckle, and odd, chewed-up pieces of rein. Finally found some ribs hangin' on the' vertebray. Part of a shoulder-blade an' leg bones. Down in a seepy willow clump finally I found an old saddle tree. Wooden parts an' iron horn. Stirrup bolts an' stirrup pieces. The cover an' skirts in curled-up pieces. Cinch rings an' old riggin' rings. Buttons an' part of an old wool coat.

"Finally figured from all th' sign that some bird had tied up his horse t' this tree a long time ago. Never come back to it."

Neeman looked around at the bunch at the table. The hunters and the rest of us were all tied up listening. Al was a real story teller. "Did you find anything more? George Parsin had started out the cook tent to hit the sack, but curiosity got the best of him. "Yeah, I did, George, but it ain't purty." Neeman was frowning down into his coffee cup. "It was clost ta noon when I found this. Got th' lunch off my horse, no use ta hunt elk fer two, three hours. Well, after I chewed on th' grub I got ta kickin' around in th' little dry park I found, where th' trees opened up. Finally found a bear trap. Sprung. With bones around. Course yuh know, mice, porkapines, coyotes, deep snow, and Nature had all worked over this whole deal. Found what I figured was parts of a grizzly. Bear claws, 'n' skull t'prove it. Human skull 'n' bones, too. Finally found rifle. Not too old a model. Lever action 1895 30-40."

"Al," I says, "is that th' old gun you've got hangin' up in your cabin?"

"Yeah, Bill, that's th' one. Plumb rusted tight. Well, I finally figured out what happened." He scratched his head and grinned. "From th' busted trap chain (had a wrench wired to it, too), and th' way th'

41

bones lay, what I could find. This man musta been a bear trapper. Caught a grizzly. Shot an' wounded him. But 'bout that time th' bear broke th' chain wired to a big tree. Killed th' man. Then died from his own wound. Horse starved t' death."

"Ever find out who th' guy was?" Shorty, next to his stove, was whittling some shavings for fire starter. Al looked around sad-like. "Nope, never did. Asked around fer years, too. Nobody I ever talked to could remember anyone missing. Musta been around 1900, I figured."

Chapter Four

It was starting to get dark by the time Al finished his story, so the two guides went down to the corral to help Slim turn the horses out. The three hunters went over to their tent. I was giving Beel a hand with his Dutch oven fire just outside the cook tent when it happened.

The wrangler, on his horse in the edge of the timber, was starting to drive the horses off while Buck and Al were shooing them out of the corral. Them 4-5 bonging clappers on the bell horses were pretty noisy; but I thought I heard a rifle shot from way off across the river above all the jangling clatter.

The biscuit-loaded Dutch oven had a broken lip on the rim. The shovel made a grating noise against it as I scraped a few more coals over on the edge. "Kinda late t' git a good shot this time o' night, ain't it?" Shorty stood in the cook tent door, holding the pot hook in his bent-up rheumatic fingers. He was peering over at the dark and shadowy cliffs, too.

"I couldn't tell whether the Ka-vroom across th' canyon was another rockslide peelin' off th' cliffs, or a shot from a high power rifle."

"Well, I thought it was a gun, too, but that jingle-jangle o' them horse bells throwed me off." Ol' Shorty turned around and bent over his cook stove. I thought, that boy's sure got a pair of ears yet, for an old throwed-out.

Back of us we could hear a couple of hunters talking in their tent— maybe they'd heard the shot, too. Sometimes in heavy timber the sound echoes from strange directions, but our camp was in a big grassy park. It was a good sound box, and the Buffalo River wasn't noisy right along here where it was flat . . . It must have come from over in the cliffs across the river.

"Well, whadda yuh know, Shorty, old boy, your nephew musta made you some teeth that fit." Tim Smithers swaggered into the lighted cook tent, and grinned down at Shorty, busy pulling brown biscuits out of the Dutch oven he'd just brought in. "Last fall, when I shot a horned owl out of that big spruce tree by the corral, your teeth fell out, and your cook fire dang near got 'em, haw, haw, haw!"

The short-coupled cook glared up. "I was a-tryin' ta ask yuh why did yuh have ta kill somethin' that wasn't a-harmin' yuh. Why, hell,

I thought I heard somebody shoot.

man, that big-eyed bird was a-killin' all the mice we git around this camp. Anybody else woulda knowed that."

Smithers came back at old Shorty with the sort of crack he loved to make. "Grinders that chawed on old bull elk meat for 40 years need better anchorage than you were givin' 'em!"

Our other two hunters came in out of the frosty night and sat down at the table. When we heard the two guides coming up, Shorty and I started to dish up the grub and get supper on the scrubbed old boards. The cook saved some back on the Rema cook stove, for the horse wrangler.

Last fall was our first acquaintance with Tim Smithers, the biggest stocks-and-bonds broker in his big town (he said). He killed a small bear, and got a pretty fair bull elk for his trophy room. All of a sudden he got a harebrained idea. He told everybody in reach that he'd pay anybody $20.00 a pair for good big bull elk teeth.

"I'm having the best tanner of the Shoshones make me a large beaded buckskin coat, and I'm going to decorate it with 1000 big elk tusks. Even Shorty is in on this deal, but I mean elk teeth, not cook's teeth, haw, haw, haw."

Johnny Beel hadn't liked that crack much. He was Shorty's nephew, in camp for a few days before he took off for dental school. He conived with Shorty to play a little joke on the broker. None of us thought Smithers was serious. And, we didn't think that dental student was, either. But you never can tell by the cover, what's in the book.

Tonight he brought up the subject again while we were eating—that Indian tanned coat with 100 elk teeth to decorate it. This got me kind of jittery. I knew by now he had lots of money and plenty of determination. "I suppose you know, Tim, that tusk-hunting is plenty illegal. Wasn't too many years ago that I knew of several gents who killed some elk for their teeth. These same smart gents ended up behind high stone walls. The spent a lot of lost time makin' horsehair bridles instead o' blowin' in easy cash from sellin' elk teeth."

What I said didn't bother that grinning hunter a danged bit. He speared another of Shorty's juicy steaks and put out his well-fed smile. "I'm just puttin' out bids. Several thousand bull elk are killed legal in these mountains every fall. Now, just where do their teeth go to? Well, I'm in the market. Good bull elk teeth only." He grinned over at the cook, who was busy rattling some split wood into the stove.

In a hunting camp the cook is the mainspring that keeps the gizzard going, and Beel was one of the best. He sure wasn't a can stabber or a baking powder bum, and besides he was a dang good friend. So I was beginning to resent Smithers' cracks at ol' Shorty. But I thought, better let it ride awhile.

Shorty wasn't even listening to that one. Buck was telling about a hunter he'd guided the year before, who wanted to keep a shell in the barrel at all times. Bruen refused to guide him unless he kept them all in the magazine until he was ready to pull down on the game. Ol' Shorty was about to shove a stick of wood into the stove.

"It's a funny thing t' me, anyhow, why a man has just *gotta* have a shell in his barrel when he's a-huntin'." The cook's piece of firewood was waving under the guide's apprehensive nose. Buck was relieved when Shorty shoved the wood in the stove, and went on, "Well, maybe not so funny, come t' remember what happened one time. Dad an' me, I was just a kid, we was camped over on Fish Creek huntin'. No game laws them days, anyways not like now. An' th' powder behind th' lead wasn't as hi-falutin as we got now; but it was just a-itchin' ta make itself felt, whether you pulled the trigger or that devil done it. Now, we was a-ridin' up this steep rocky draw. Dry, no snow. We knowed they was a bunch of elk in th' basin at th' head of th' draw. Gonna make a quick sneak on 'em, Dad said, Git th' job done. Three or four anyhow. About halfway up this rocky draw, Dad jist ahead o' me, both of us leanin' over our horses' necks, helpin' 'em climb kinda, well, it happened. We was all four of us busy, I can tell yuh. But all of a sudden when that gun went off we got a damn sight busier. My dad's horse, about t' go around past a big dead tree down crosswise of the game trail we was climbin'—he rared dang nigh straight up an' tried t' jump over the snaggy log. Well, Dad swapped his saddle f'r a mess a boulders without any boot. My nag, busy dodgin' rollin' rocks anyhow, whirled around before I knowed it, and headed down, me see-sawing my 16-year-old best on them reins. I got him stopped jist as he was about t' put a big puddin' foot on my new 30-30 I'd got for trappin' beaver that spring. Th' smoke was still comin' outa th' barrel, it happened so quick. But I seen an' felt more smoke, in a head-shrinkin' sort o' way, right sudden. That Dad o' mine wasn't tongue-tied, I can tell you.

"By th' time we'd ontangled th' bleedin' horse outa that tangled-up bunch a limbs an' rocks, an' was back down t' th' tent, doctorin' him up, I had a new education. An' th' mental part is still stickin'. My old Dad had told me a thousand times, he says, '*Never* keep a load in th' barrel. If you *ain't got time* t' throw one in th' chamber when yer onta game, you *ain't got time* ta git a shot anyways.'" Shorty was waving a spoon now. "Well, the strap on th' back end of my scabbard

All of a sudden, the gun went off.

broke an' my loaded rifle slid out. It musta lit on a rock, and bang! That horse got a crease on *his* rump, an' I got a lump on mine."

Ol' Shorty had the whole gang laughing at his long-ago story, but I was a-hopin' that story would stick in these hunters' minds. You never can tell a trigger-happy bird by the feathers he's wearing or the song he sings.

We were just cleaning up on the peach pie when we heard a horse trotting up the trail, and the little humming song Slim always had on tap. When we heard the pounding of the axe as the wrangler drove in a green stake on fresh grass for the night horse, Shorty started to put Slim's grub on the table. We could hear him over at the gear tent putting his saddle and outfit away. Soon he was swooshing and gasping as he washed up in the cold water at the wash block outside in the dark. He stooped to get his long frame into the cook tent door, and stood grinning down at the cook as he warmed his hands over the Rema stove. He laughed when the hunters kidded him about his icy habit of cold water. "Horse jinglin' in this altitude at night is a sleepy job. Too easy. You can't beat mountain water."

The crowd slid over and made way for Slim to get at the supper that Shorty had all dished for him. He just got started to eat, when suddenly he stopped. "Just happened to think, when I started to run our horse bunch away from the corral, I thought I heard somebody shoot. Did you fellers hear a shot?"

Shorty was starting to wash dishes. He stopped and looked around at me. "Yeah, me an' Bill thought we did, too. Couldja tell where it come from?"

"My horse bells was making such a racket I couldn't get the directions," Slim says. "Prob'ly just some elk hunter shootin' shadows in th' dark."

Dr. Forrester puts in, "George and Tim and I all thought we heard a shot, too, but we had our tent flap tied down. We couldn't tell where it came from, either."

Tim Smithers, like always the loud-talking man from the big city, claimed that if a sound came from the north, he knew, from all his experience in the mountains, that it was actually from the south.

Buck and Al were helping Shorty clean up the supper, and rattling the tin plates, pots, and pans at a great rate, while the talk went on about the way sounds carry and echo in the mountains. Slim wasn't saying a word, just forking food into his gullet and grinning down at his plate.

I knew now it must have been a shot fired somewhere that night.

Everybody was ready to hit the sack. As the three hunters started to leave for their own tent, Tim said, "Well, if that shot means somebody's lost, it's the survival of the fittest, here on these hills or on the sidewalks of New York. Maybe somebody sneaked up on a big bull elk that had good-lookin' teeth a-shinin' in the dark, haw, haw!

Buck Bruen lingered to tell us about George Parsin. He was kinda disgusted. "Naw, Shorty, we didn't get a thing, but wait'll I tell yuh: Parsin an' me was ridin' along on them benches above th' mouth o' Cub Creek. Heard a bull elk bugle down in them quaking aspen. We tied up our horses for a look-see, and George got his rifle, while I walked over a couple hundred feet t' look down in a little grassy park.

"A real good six-point was right in th' middle of this park, six or seven cows an' a couple calf elk feedin' in back of him, close t' them rimrocks above 'em. I made sign an' hid behind a big tree. George, he made a good sneak through th' open pine timber. Him an' that big bull elk saw each other at th' same time. Th' bull was puttin' out big wheezy grunts, an' slashin' at a little green spruce, but when he saw Parsin aimin' at him, he quit. He just starts walkin' kinda stiff-legged, gruntin' an' hostile, towards George, up above him an' in the trees. Them cows an' calves stopped feedin', an' the damn fools stood an' watched their bull. They musta not seen that hunter or me." Bruen snorted. "I was waitin' for George t' shoot. When he saw that sappy bull start towards him, he lowered his gun, don't even look at me. He walked back to his horse, put th' rifle back in the' scabbard. The' bull stopped an' put his head close t' th' ground and whistled. Them cows still standin' there. Me, I'm about t' come apart!

"While me an' them silly cow elk are still in a daze, that hunter comes over with his *movie camera* an' turns that whizzin' thing loose. What happens then, y' say, Shorty? Why, hell! Nuthin'! When that nut runs outa them film, that Barrymore bull an' his silly cows git spooked 'n' take t' th' timber. Me, I'm jist th' guide.

"When we untie th' horses, I ain't said a word yet. Couldn't. Parsin says, 'Say, Buck, you've got the politest elk I ever heard of.' 'Think nothin' of it,' I tells him, 'Wyoming elk don't ever see any damfools in th' fall. Hardly ever.' Say, Bill," Buck, was scratching his ear and looking out across the dark to the hunter's lighted tent, "I kinda like that there Parsin."

Well, we all got snuggled down for the night. The three hunters had a wall tent to themselves, Buck and Al had a big tepee close to the cook tent. Big Slim bunked in the gear tent, said he felt at home in with the pack saddles and the sacks of grain.

The Barrymore bull.

Shorty and I had our bedrolls back of the table in the cook tent. Just after Shorty wound his 4 a.m. alarm clock, and was squirming and grunting into his rolled-out bed, it came again. I had just faintly heard some wheezy bull elk bugling their brags to the frosty stars back up on Terrace Mountain, so I wasn't sure. The cook stopped rattling the bed tarp, and I heard some mumbling over in the guides' tepee. "That sure ain't no rock fallin' that time, that *was* a shot. Somebody must be strayed or lost," Shorty was sure about it.

"Hey, Bill," Slim stood outlined in the cold moonlight in his long underwear and boots, his wool shirt humped around his lanky carcass. "Somebody has got lost up around them cliffs. Didja hear that shot?"

"Yeah, me an' Shorty heard it, too. We'll have t'take a sashay over there in the mornin'. Break our necks tryin' ta negotiate in there tonight. Say, grab that 95 Winchester of mine on th' table top, an' shoot three times t' let him know we hear him." I reared up half outa my bed roll and snapped on a flashlight for Slim. He levered a shell in and fired a shot at the stars, then twice again.

We all listened for a long time, while Slim shivered in the frosty night, but heard no answering shot. The hunters and guides hollered out of their tents for the news, then after a while we all settled down for an uneasy snooze. Don't take long till morning in a hunting camp, no matter how early you roll in.

51

Chapter Five

Next morning we had our horses saddled before daylight. I'll say this for that tall horse wrangler, he always run the horses in plenty early, and no never mind at that. He always beat the cook up, and no noise either. Anyway, we rode across the river and up into that rocky cut-up scrub timber just under the cliffs, the whole seven of us, hunters, guides, and Slim. Ramblin' around spread out, we shot a few times and hollered a lot, then finally located a scratched-up and half-frozen hunter hunched up close by a cabin-sized boulder, over a smoky fire he'd got going. He was O.K., outside of a sprained ankle, an empty belly, and a powerful yen for some shut-eye. He had a rifle, but was out of ammunition.

Slim got him loaded on his saddle horse, and walked off, leading the pony carrying the dilapidated hunter. I knew the wrangler would get back to camp; he was humming that little tune and grinning as he picked their way down through the jungle of rocks.

Well, we split up after that. Buck and Al elected to take their hunters in different directions to prospect for elk. So Mr. Elk Tooth and yours truly headed over through some scrub jungle to the big parks above the Cub Creek rims. A good spot to maybe nail one of those big throwed-out bulls.

An elk bugled way up at the head of a steep grassy draw we were about to cross. We had just quit the heavy timber, and were riding down this steep game trail, when Smithers' horse gave a loud snort and ran slam-bang up against mine. Above Tim's furious cussing and the mixup of horses, I could hear "Yee-ough, Yee-ough," real loud and plenty close—a cow elk barking. That bond broker's horse whirled around and dang near knocked old Roany out from under me, then he started to gallop back up the trail, with old Elk Tooth cussing and see-sawing on the reins. The big field glasses strapped to Tim's neck hadn't kept up with the times; they were now hammering the hunter on both shoulder blades. The big rifle under Tim's leg started to come backwards out of the scabbard. When I saw about a foot of daylight between that big rump and the busy saddle, with the rifle telescope trying to pick up the pieces. But about then his fool horse stopped dead still, snorting and blowing at the crowd in front of him.

Scratched up and half frozen.

We were surrounded by a bunch of elk, it looked like. Up on both sides of the draw, in the edge of the timber, ten or twelve cow elk stood, bugging their eyes right back at ours. The few calves with them couldn't believe their eyes, either. But that silly old maid, somewhere in the timber close by, finally "Yee-oughed" loud enough to make 'em believe it. A few snorts and snuffy whistles, and we were along again. "That crazy dam sucker," was all Smithers had to say, by the time we got organized again.

In an hour or so, we located a big antlered old grunter and had the wind right, but that stocks and bonds magnate missed two easy shots. I found a couple of playful pine needles wedged in the front of the telescope sight. Then I had to stop the infuriated hunter from busting his four-hundred-dollar musket across a big rock. Can happen to anybody. Some days you can't make a dime, not even a ten-cent bond. He didn't love nobody by the time we walked back to our saddle horses.

We were circling through the timber, when a sudden squalling clamor of Clark's crows and whisky jacks drew us to a sight that made Moneybags grin. It brought back that uneasy feeling to me. There was reason enough for the gobbling racket of the shiny black ravens and the joyful screeching of the other birds. A couple coyotes trotted up the slope, looking back at us, then disappeared into the trees.

As we sat our horses in the long black shadows from the heavy timber behind us, the sun threw shutters of yellow light past us and on to the steep grassy hillside below. The carpet of gold light sloped on down toward Cub Creek, its beauty marred by the torn-up remains of five elk. Dozens of birds were in a frenzy of screaming delight at the clean-up job on four of the elk carcasses; while a huge old golden eagle, all by his lonesome, clumsily trundled around yanking shreds off the farthest one, a forlorn remnant of an elk calf close to the canyon's dropoff.

We worked our way down off the ledgy rimrock, got off our jittery horses, tied them up to trees, and walked over to look at this massacre. Two cow elk with their calves, and a young spike two-year-old, had been shot and left lay. But when I walked around the carnage, the birds jealously watching from nearby treetops, I found eight chopped-off big elk legs, scattered around in the heavy grass. Near as I could figure, the signs showed somebody had packed off two bull elk, and left the other five. Then I looked some more, and found that the tusks of the two big cows had been dug out. The tusks of the spike elk hadn't been touched. They're usually just a hollow shell. The vandals knew their grisly business.

A frenzy of screaming delight.

I looked over at my hunter. He sat on a big rock now, a sly grin on his big aggressive jaw. "Dog eat dog," he says, "and the devil take the hindmost." He waved a huge paw all around the scene. Well, that hunch, I've got a built-in one now, feels like what old Doc Rep says is an amateur ulcer just a-feelin' its oats in the fall.

We got back on our horses. While we were picking our way down through the jungly blowdowns towards the mouth of Cub Creek, I got to ruminating on this deal. Old bull elk stay by themselves at this rutting time of the year; at least that's the way I know it. Seems the lusty young bulls throw out some of these lecherous old boys. They may have passed their prime of virility, but their horns still seem to be as staunch and tremendous as their bodies used to be. They mumble along by themselves, sometimes tagged by an understudy or two of admiring spike elk. Sometimes grunting old grandpa picks up sympathetically with another wheezing big-horned old stinker, and they tromp from park to jungle, bugling their loud frustration from swamp to peak and back again. A lot of these bulls may have only their imagination left, but most of them have fine big tusks along with that huge rack of horns. Lots of times their remains are found on windswept ridges. Sometimes in mild winters they survive. It's risky for the ones who are overcome by optimism and elect to stay all winter up high. If the wind blows off enough snow so they can paw for enough feed, maybe they won't have to drift to lower altitudes. But the bark on quaking apsens and other trees sometimes gives out along with the browse. The deep snow foils their instinct to paw down. Their luck gives out right there. Goodbye, old wapiti.

Thinking of tusks of dead elk: usually hunters take them from their own legally killed animals. Human wanderers in the mountain country, summer and fall, sometimes come across the skeletons of winter-killed wapiti. They see the tusks in dried-out, coyote-drug skulls. They pry them out, to polish and treasure back home. Other times, elk meet with a natural accident; or are wounded, and cripple away to die unseen—it happens, even when the hunters are conscientious and try to find them. Most of the times it's hard to tell, when you find them, whether they've died of old age, natural causes, or found too late; though sometimes shattered bones tell of a bullet.

In these last few years, most of the carcasses I'd run across were elk; hardly ever deer, mountain sheep, or moose. Mostly elk. And in nearly every case the tusks were gone. Whether I found them in jungle pockets, on windswept ridges, or in grassy open valleys, these empty sockets told no tales. I'm no Sherlock Holmes in chaps, and most detectives don't have bow legs; but that hunch was with me just the same.

Well, it was nearly dark by the time we got to the park where camp was. The horse bunch had been turned out, for we could hear the belled ones jangle the direction they fed, over in the grassy park. I grained our two at the corral, for Slim to turn out late. I could hear Tim Smithers talking with the other hunters in their tent as I stumbled throught the grassy pine needles toward the lighted cook tent. I passed Slim's saddle horse tied to a tree by the corral. I noticed again that he had a halter and rope tied behind the saddle. May be a thrifty habit.

Buck and Al were helping Shorty clear up the camp table to put on supper for Smithers and me. Everybody else had got in early and were already finished. Slim left, and rode out to throw the last two saddle horses in with the grazing horse bunch.

"Your grub's too good, Shorty," Smithers loved to razz the cook. "This morning Bill had to help me get on my horse." "Yeah." Beel looked him over. "That bay window looks bad. I'll put rocks in yer biscuits from now on."

While Tim and I ate our supper, the boys told us the happenings. George Parsin downed a big bull elk a couple of hours after we'd all split up under the cliff, Buck said; and Al Neeman's hunter, Doc Forrester, missed a running shot at an enormous black bear; and late in the afternoon a couple of searchers came to camp looking for the lost hunter, and went back to their camp with him. They'd brought a led saddle horse, just in case.

Well, I finally told the boys what Tim Smithers and I saw on the hill above Cub Creek, after the hunters had gone back to their tent, and Shorty was slicking up his pots and pans for the night. He and the guides were all mountain men who had traveled these mountains for years same as I had. Al Neeman, sixtyish, and tough as a moose, says, "Sounds like some a th' new style hunters we got nowadays. Made what they call a drive. Killed too many, like a lot of them game hogs. Looks like th' game department oughta wake up. Them big tecknishuns won't have any animals left t' write them beautiful reports about."

Old Buck Bruen, helping Shorty, wipes the last tin plate and gets his say in: "Yeah, a lot of our game wardens are hard working and good men on th' job. But some a th' ones we drawed around these parts are home every night in th' fancy houses Game-and-Fish built for 'em. They stay where th' people are, not where th' game is. Badge polish don't shine up a saddle like use does. Bed rolls an' tents let in more drafts than gas-heated houses with beds built for beauty-rest. I'm not delicate, so that job'll never be mine."

"Couldja figger how long them elk had been killed?" Shorty was stacking split wood behind the Rema stove.

"Musta been a week ago anyhow, near as I can guess by th' sign. Them chopped-off legs show that two big bull elk was killed right there, too; they'd been packed out. But th' ones that was left wasn't touched. Only th' cows, and they only took tusks offa them. A slaughter, an' they only used two outa the whole bunch."

We could hear the horse wrangler as he picketed his horse to a loose log. Now he stooped to come into the cook tent. He heard part of my last remarks, so I told him about the whole deal. He eased his lanky frame down on a saw block by the cook stove. "You say the teeth were taken out of those two cows? And the others left? If there's much of that goin' on, Wyoming'll be outa elk in a few years."

Old Buck chipped in, "Well, boys, everybody has got his own way t'hunt and his own ideas about how t' git onta game, any kind. We all know that. But when it gets so that people start t' ambush game like this deal was done, it's time fer some hell t' be raised. Legal or otherwise. If the game department don't start doin' somethin' about mass murder, the people will hafta."

Shorty was putting his sourdough keg to bed. He wrapped a towel around it, then an old coat. Now he got in his say: "I fed that lost hunter Slim brought in this morning, and put him t' bed in my rig. After he got a lot a shut-eye, he rolled out about noon, an' he and Slim an' me, we ate dinner, an' he give us th' lowdown on how he got mislaid last night. I don't reckon, from th' way he was teed off, that th' outfitter he was a-huntin' with'll be collectin' any dough f'r his hunt. If that's what yuh could call it.

"He said, yesterday four-five outa state hunters includin' him rode outa their camp with th' outfitter, th' wrangler, an' two guides. Well, this hunter says, th' whole outfit rode up a steep trail through a lotta timber, an' come out on them high timbered benches where they could see clear around th' country. He musta been up there above that slide rock country back of where we heard him shoot last night. The gent gits madder'n madder while he's tellin' us this yarn. Anyhow, th' boss 'n' his hands spot 8 or 10 head a elk down under this rim they're a-watchin' from. In a kinda pocket like. This gang o' big game guides stations him an' th' other city hunters on different spots about two or three hundred yards apart, all around a kind of natural pass. Tells 'em all t' stay hid, like. Tells 'em they, th' guides, are goin' ta ride down

58

behind that buncha elk. Also th' outfitter says, 'Them there elk'll come through this pass here, when we an' th' boys git behind 'em t' spook 'em out.' He says, 'Give 'em hell, men. You c'n git th' whole bunch. Take yore pick,' he says, 'don't be bashful.' An' then they ride off down inta them breaks. Well, he waited an' waited, nuthin' happened. He stayed put for four or five hours, damn near froze, didn't hear a sound, not even a chipmunk, wore his eyes out a-watchin' th' pass, didn't hear a shot. Couldn't see where his feller sportsmen was stationed, prob'ly stayin' put, too, waitin' fer th' elk that was a-goin' ta come through the pass."

Slim was grinning at Shorty, telling the hunter's story. He nodded his head. "Yep, that's th' way he told it, all right. Before he got done he got hungry again, and Shorty had ta stoke him up, to hear about th' rest of his big elk hunt. Sure got weak when he got mad at th' way forty dollars a day was th' rate t' get lost."

Shorty puts in, "Anyhow, it gits dark on him, an' he shoots two-three times but gits no answer. He figgers he kin git back t' that stretch of timber where they'd tied up all th' sports saddle horses. If they've left him, mebbe his horse'll take him back t' camp. He stumbles around, darker'n hell, cloudy 'n' no moon t' see by, falls over rocks an' runs inta trees. Figgers mebbe he's close t' th' horses when he hears some snorts—prob'ly was that band of elk they didn't get. Finally takes a hard fall in a rocky willa bog. Can't see, no moon yet, but his ankle is sprained. Loses his rifle, then fumbles around an' steps on it, gits scared, fires th' shots we hear down here last night. Finally hears ol' Slim shootin'. Then he figgers he better stay put, when he finds he's lost his extry shells. Stays all night up there an' then you find him. Sure lucky, he says, but ta hell with huntin' elk if that's th' way it's done."

Me and this crew of mine talked awhile about this ruckus, thinking of all the hunters lost in the mountains, ones we knew about and others we'd heard of. Our hunter, Hackett, had lost himself, while this stranger we'd collected had his hard luck through the dumb tactics of a crooked outfitter. When ol' Shorty said, "Looks like th' Man up above was a-watchin' both a them gents; them fellers coulda got inta worse jams than they did." We all agreed with those sentiments, and then decided to hit the sack, too.

I couldn't sleep for quite a long time. No, I didn't start counting sheep; I was counting elk, but the way things were stacking up, I figured I was going to run out of elk, and maybe would have to stay awake all night. Old Shorty's rattling snores flopped the tent flap, but

Elk walking along single file.

didn't bother me. What did jitter me was his scattered mumbling about big elk teeth, so I had to try to think of something else.

I shoved the blankets and tarp to one side and lifted up the bottom edge of the tent wall. No clouds. It was bright moonlight now. Looking past the frost on the tent rope and pegs, I could see Slim's night horse, tied with a long rope to a loose log. Once in a while he'd quit grazing, throw up his head, and listen, lonesome-like, to the far-off horse bells on some of our horse bunch over across the Buffalo on the grassy benches. Then, big as a elephant, a mouse humped along past the forest of tent ropes, pegs, frosty grass blades, and distant tree trunks. After he left, I was getting frosty myself around the withers. I was about to lower the curtain on this show when, way off, past the glittering grass tops, I caught sight of two or three cow elk walking along single file toward the river. A big bull was in the rear.

All I could see was their bodies from the belly up. The moon cast silvery glints of light on the big boy's antlers, and on the body outlines of the darker cows. I could even hear the faint clattery splashes of young ice broken, as they disappeared over the river to the dark spruce jungle beyond.

Well, we got a few elk left, anyhow, I figured. At some more elk teeth mumbles from over in the dreaming cook's bed roll, I dropped the canvas edge on the ground, and drug the stiff tarp over my head; elk teeth or stomach ulcers, here I come! But even then, I was a-doin' it again; so I got a new line of thought; and there it was, all elk. The fact is, I thought, when the moon is full like now, the elk feed at night, and mostly leave the grassy parks by early morning. Then they go back into the timbered jungles to chew their cuds, rest, and ruminate on the perfidy of all mankind, until in early evening when they get hungry again; all this depending on their appetite and the kind of feed they're on.

Oh, sure, some big-headed old bull, throwed out of the harem by some smart and tough young upstart, gets foolish ideas and crosses open spots going from one stretch of timber to another. He's looking for a grass-widow elk; but not finding any unattached, he grazes along timbered fringes of meadow, bugling and grunting in angry perplexity. Also, sons or stepsons, spike elk, tag along or try to. And some old maid elk looking for sympathetic company may stray absent-mindly across openings. So hunting elk in the fall (if you get trophy heads) seems to me either plain happenstance luck, or knowledge and strategy and skill at outwitting. This gang killing is foreign to most people's instincts, I thought; and with that I musta dropped off.

Chapter Six

We started out after daylight the next morning. Smithers had spend half the night cleaning his two-eyed fancy blunderbuss. He went out with old Buck Bruen, whose hunter had got a big-headed elk yesterday. They'd packed it in, and the meat was now cooling off on the meat pole back of the tents. Buck told me privately that Slim didn't need anybody's help on packing. "That guy slung them elk quarters an' horns on them two horses slicker'n a whistle, an' throwed as good a diamond as any hand I ever worked with. He didn't need me at all." Now Buck's hunter, George Parsin, wanted to try for a bear; so he and I rode off together, after we talked over with the other guides our plans of where we were going.

As we rode through a stretch of lodgepole timber, I got to thinking about how Slim Wilson was handling our horse bunch. His quiet self-assurance and his friendly ways were easy to get along with. He was darned good with horses, and it was turning out that he could pack and shoe with the best of them. He never talked much about himself and claimed to be a stranger around these parts. He made comments about packing and hunting in Idaho, but that was about all. He'd been running the horse bunch in before daylight. After we had the horses we were going to use that day, he'd keep the rest of them in the corral for four or five hours, then run them out on good feed until evening. Then he'd bring 'em in to grain up. When we had all come in, he'd put our saddle horses with the bunch, and then locate the whole bunch on new grass for the night. When I kidded him about the halter behind his cantle, he said there seemed to be a bunch-quitter or two in our string. Slim said he missed one or two lone feeders when he rounded them up in the dark early morning. After we'd got our hunting horses out, and left after breakfast, he'd ride out and locate the lost one, catch him, and lead him in to the corral to put with the bunch. That was reasonable, all right, but I noticed the three or four wrangle horses he'd changed off on seemed to be rode down more than they should be. He took good care of 'em, though, and grained 'em plenty. As we were riding off this morning, Shorty was cleaning up around the cook tent and Slim was busy at the wood pile, so I reckoned the horse bunch was all there.

I'd noticed bear sign up by those elk carcasses above Cub Creek the day before. Parsin and I got up there pretty late, but we did see a big black bear and her two cubs having the time of their lives trying to put the run on the birds yelling around. No soap on a mamma with kids. But the big buck deer in a stand of quaking aspens didn't have a chance. George Parsin nailed him first shot. I dressed him out and throwed him on my big roan. George rode ahead and I walked, leading old Roany and his fresh load. Maybe in the morning we'd find a new bear on the buck's entrails back there. Good bear country up there by the Buffalo Falls.

We tied our horses and ate lunch in the shadow of a clump of lodgepole pine. Sitting in the dry grass, leaning up against a big limby deadfall, George says, in between bites of Shorty's juicy sandwiches, "Smithers is sure enough set on having those elk teeth, isn't he? Must have a lot of dough to go with such onery ideas. If the wrong kind of money-hungry birds try to supply him, they all ought to land in jail."

"Th' game laws say that no edible portion of game meat can be sold or bartered," I says, "but that lets out tusks. I don't reckon Tim can find any jackass dumb enough to kill elk for their teeth. Like you say, they could both git years in the hoosegow for that, if caught. Don't see how he can contact enough hunters or owners of legal teeth, either."

"Those elk carcasses we saw the bear family chasing the birds off of, what do you make of that?"

"Could be that somebody got too excited when they run onta that bunch of elk. Trigger-happy gents, maybe. Killed 'em all before they realized what got into 'em, then they got scared. They come back, though, an' packed out th' two bulls; I'd a taken the' cows myself. Better meat. But they did rob th' cows o' their tusks, an' that's what bothers me."

While we were talking, I was glassing the country with Parsin's powerful binoculars. Might pick out some bear snoopin' around out in the open. I caught just a blurry movement of something through some tree clumps across the South Fork, over close to where the elk carcasses lay. Boy, those glasses were powerful. Sure like to have that pair. We were around two miles from the grassy slope above Cub Creek. . . . But there he was. It was the wrangler, a long ways from camp, riding the big snorty buckskin. He was staying in the shadows of the timber, but now and then a sunny spot would show him riding slowly around, in and out of the trees above the dead elk, and he wasn't leading any lost horse.

Our two horses tied just behind us started snorting and faunching around. When I lowered the glasses to look, a big brown bear was just disappearing up through a heavy growth of spruce. Parsin was right on the ball; he had his rifle up, aiming, but he was a little too late. That brown was sure fanning his ears. He was in a hell of a hurry.

Goerge had a big grin on his angular face when he slowly lowered his rifle and looked around at me. "That bear wants my buck deer, not his entrails back there. But he doesn't seem to chase us kind of birds away from the meat . . . Bill, just before the bear broke up our lunch hour, I was about to ask you if game wardens ever come up into this part of the mountains."

"You know, that's what bothers me. Years ago, when I started huntin' 'n' guidin' in this here same country, they would show up pretty often. Mostly they were ex-guides an' packers. I knew a lot of 'em and sure liked to have 'em around. They knew th' game an' the mountains an' all their ways. I ain't had any game wardens check any o' my hunters or camps for a long time now."

"When we stopped down in Roaring River, the day we came to the ranch, seemed like there were quite a few game wardens in town, and I talked with several of them. They seemed like fine, upstanding young fellows."

"Yeah, the ones I know are. Lots of 'em are able game wardens; but in th' old days you'd meet em out in th' hills more 'n y' would in town."

It was dark by the time we got into camp, what with George lallygagging around with short stops taking pictures. Then it was too late to get the best picture, Parsin said, of the whole trip. For in front of the cook tent was Tim Smithers seated on a block of firewood, and in the light of the big campfire was Buck Bruen, grinning and pouring iodine on the big hunter's bowed head. As we came closer to look, Buck let the bottle slip, accidental like, and some of the stuff trickled down in the back of Smithers' shirt, and must have went pretty far down, for he jumped up with a big yelp and grabbed himself.

Shorty was standing in the door of the cook tent holding the gas lantern for Buck to see better. He cackled an old man's giggle, "I'll betcha that big horned owl that tried to scalp ya t'night was cousin ta the one you shot outa that spruce tree last fall."

Smithers grimaced over in Shorty's direction and surprised us all with, "Let the punishment fit the crime."

We found that Buck and the stocks-and-bonds man had got to camp just a little before we did. Out in the big park, Tim had rode under a low tree limb and had his hat brushed off. A big swoopy flash of wings, and whango! a horned owl out hunting for supper mistook that white head bobbing along beneath him for a snowshoe rabbit. All he got was a shreddy clawful of outraged white hair. Buck, riding ahead in the dark, said he didn't know a leading millionaire could scream such horrible lowbrow bad words.

Smithers was sure defensive at supper. If he even thought anyone was looking at his dyed head, he'd switch the conversation around to his so-called achievements. Doc Forrester wondered at the fact that there were no wolves left in this part of the country, nothing in the dog line but coyotes and some red foxes. Smithers had the answer for this one. "They all went to the big cities," he cracks. "It's dog eat dog, there, if they're tryin' to make big money. It takes a wolf to catch a wolf, no panty-waist coyotes there. And me, I've got the best and biggest business of its kind in my town."

After he went to his tent, George Parsin and Doc Forrester lingered over more coffee with the bunch. Looked like they got a band out of the comments on Smithers' declaration. Al poured himself some more java. "Shore, shore, when this rich yak-yak kicks that golden bucket, he'll have a newer and bigger tombstone put on his grave each year. Prob'ly leave that pervision in his will." Slim, he never says a dad-blamed word about all the deal. Just swigs coffee and grins. Finally, before we all turned in, Buck has his say: "In old Full-pockets' game of put and take, I'll bctcha he's gotta cinch up his light *put* side o' th' pack a damn sight tighter 'n th' *take*."

The next day we all saw game but no trophy heads; except Doc Forrester and Al Neeman. The good doctor had no trouble getting in one good shot which done the business, according to Al. Neeman's little brown eyes twinkled when he told us, "You'd oughta heard him namin' all the innards while I cleaned out his elk. The hell of it was, they was all in Latin or somethin', longest tongue-twistin' I ever heard. I told Doc, I could clean out a critter without them big words; but if a M.D. had t'know words like them t' put th' innards back in so's they'd work, why, I was sure gonna stay jist a guide."

That evening Dr. Forrester and Smithers caught a few trout in the big bend of the Buffalo, just below camp. Tim spied a large cow moose in the edge of some heavy timber; he laid his fishing rod down and unlimbered his camera. Sneaking in closer for a better shot, he ended up climbing a tree when the moose charged him. Doc had to rescue him by thowing rocks at the jealous mother. Forrester said, "I never did see the calf, but I knew there was one back in the trees."

"You birds sure had a streak of luck, when that cow moose went back to her calf," Slim Wilson told them. "If it had been spring, and that calf was plumb new, I'll bet you'd a had a jangle. Over in Idaho, one time, a moose cow, with a new addition in th' family, didn't like publicity. She musta figured her baby was either too snooty or too homely to have its picture taken. Anyhow, I was drivin' down th' highway a few miles below th' ranch I was workin' for, headed for town. Come to a big bend along th' river, timber 'n' willow bottoms on both sides. I saw a new-lookin' car parked a few feet off this oiled road, and there was a screamin' woman alone in it. I stopped my pickup an' looked around. Couldn't see another soul, until I happened t' look down th' steep grade to the river's edge. There was a big cow moose standin' on her hind legs in th' water, strikin' a man with her front feet. She had 'im pawed down to his knees on th' bank. Her squealin' an' them huffy grunts had that hollerin' woman in th' car beat all to thunder. This bird wasn't sayin' a word, but he didn't seem t' be enjoyin' this kind of affection. So I jumpted outa th' pickup an' ran down there, grabbin' up a short tree limb a-layin' in th' rocks. I whunked this mad female on her snoot a time or two. She whirled around an' splashed back across th' river, to a calf I saw, barely hidden in the willows over there. I helped this gashed-up gent to his feet, and finally got his wobbly carcass back up th' grade to his car.

"Naw, his wife'd quit screamin', but she never did get outa th' car. Too scared t'move, I reckon. You know, this gent finally sorta come to when he got close t' his car. He suddenly jumped in th' driver's seat, started up th' motor, an' took off down th' road. Nope, neither him or his old lady said a word all this time. Them nature lovers didn't say howdy, kiss me, go t' hell or even goodbye, just took off in a hell of a hurry down th' road.

"About that time, wonderin' if I was goin' deef, dumb, or blind, I sorta come out of it, an' curious about why th' man an' th' moose got into this jamboree in th' first place. So I walked back down to th' battlefield. I looked over cross th' river, but that bogtrotter wasn't in sight. Then I saw something glisten in th' roily water. I fished around with a stick until I hooked out th' sad remains of a stomped-up camera. When I got back t' my pickup an' started her up, I got ta thinkin', sometimes it pays t' ask first."

Smithers took all this in with a big grin. "Well, if any long nose sucker like that one ever chases me up a tree again, I'll start collecting moose teeth, too."

66

She had him pawed down to his knees.

Chapter Seven

Next day started out about as usual, with nothing happening out of the ordinary. But when we got back to camp after dark, I found that something had happened there that changed the whole hunting camp to something else. Pete Elaby had packed in some supplies we'd been looking for, and brought the accumulated mail—and little Sally!

Al Neeman told me about it. "By golly, Bill," Neeman was squinting at me, "Doc went out with Slim 'n me t' git movies while we packed his elk in. He run outa film f'r his camery. We wasn't far f'm camp, so I come in with him t' git some more."

Forrester and Parsin had gone over to their tent, and Buck was helping the wrangler stack some sacks of grain in the gear tent. We could hear Shorty out in the dark throwing some cans into the garbage pit. "I hope Johnnie ain't in some jam, back east, Bill." Al had a hoarse whisper. "I figure on him doin' my grinder work some day." From the lighted tent we could hear Shorty's shovel scrape on the rocks at the pit back in the timber, and Slim's and Buck's voices over in the gear tent.

"I saw Sally holdin' Shorty by th' wrist and talkin' like a Dutch uncle. She was shakin' her finger under th' ol' boy's nose, an' boy, was she mad!" Al kept looking furtively out into the black night. "I saw all this while I was helpin' Pete pack Parsin's meat an' heads on them jacks of his. Ol' Shorty wasn't sayin' much an' he sure was listenin' close t' that mad little Indian." Neeman stopped to listen again, then he said, "All I could git outa th' deal was 'city slickers!' She hissed it real loud a coupla times. Sally was shakin' her head at somethin' Shorty was sayin', she was holdin' Shorty by th' wrist by one hand an' th' other was held straight back of her. Looked like at letter she was holdin'." Al was getting excited. He kept listening to make sure Shorty was still covering up the garbage." "Bill, all of a sudden, th' cook made a grab and got that letter outa Sally's hand, and that little Injun slapped him one alongside th' jaw, an' kinda wailed, 'Oh! Uncle Shorty!' Then ol' Shorty kinda trotted up towards th' cook tent. Nope, he didn't say a word, jist kinda mumbles somethin', didn't even look back at that poor kid.

"What did she do? Why, she jist turned around an' run up t' her

She slapped him alongside the jaw.

horse, grazin' over close t' th' corral. She was up on that surprised critter like a flash an' was poppin' him on th' belly, lopin' down th' trail an' outa sight before y' could say Geronimo!"

About that time the cook come back into the tent, and that's all I got outa Al. He sure ain't no stool pigeon, and he thinks a lot of old Shorty, so I figured this must be another one of them dang belly wobblers. The cook didn't mention Sally's visit, and I didn't ask.

While we were eating breakfast next morning, Shorty was sure grumpy. "What's the matter, old boy, did a mouse fall into your sourdough keg last night?" "Sure did, Tim," Shorty gives Smithers a grunt, "Cantcha notice th' taste?" Didn't bother old Elk-Tooth a bit. He just grins, and snares another golden cake, and dribbles syrup on it, for answer.

Slim put in, "You shoulda seen th' show in th' gear tent last night. Somethin' woke me up and I snapped on my flashlight. A big snowshoe rabbit was at th' foot of my bedroll, eatin' oats out of a hole in a grain sack, and perched right up above him was two white-footed mice a-watchin'. They musta give up an' come over to the cook tent." Doc Forrester asked if the gear tent put on any other shows. Slim had a good one: "Night before last a loud thumping woke me up. I grabbed for my flashlight, but something had a-holt of it. Finally I won the struggle, and there under a pack saddle was a big pack rat. He made a last desperate grab for the flashlight, but he seen I was the biggest, so he thumped a time or two, and took off, mad as hell. Mebbe his eyes are haywire. It sure gets dark in these mountains." The hunters and the rest of us had to laugh at Slim's description of all the activity in the gear tent, but Beel didn't seem to get any bang out of it.

We didn't go hunting till afternoon that day. The hunters all decided they had to write letters that morning. Pete Elaby was due in again with supplies from the ranch. He'd take our mail back in with him to send from Roaring River, and the rest of the meat and trophy heads we had accumulated.

When I saw ol' Shorty fumbling around in his private set of rawhide panniers at the back of the cook tent, I recollected the letter from Velma I'd taken off the cook table last night and stuck in my pocket. I was too tired to read it then. I pulled it out, and went to sit on the wash block in the sun:

Dear Bill,

Things are going all right here at the ranch. I hope the list of supplies and the things the hunters wanted sent out to camp are all

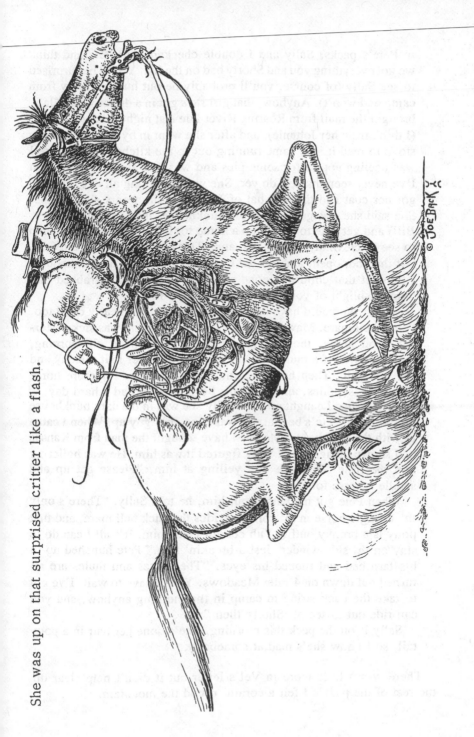

She was up on that surprised critter like a flash.

in Pete's packs. Sally and I double checked with Pete and think
we got everything you and Shorty had on the list. You'll be surprised
to see Sally (of course, you'll probably be out hunting away from
camp and won't). Anyhow, that girl *sure* got in a dither when Elaby
brought the mail from Roaring River late last night. She got a letter
(I think from her Johnnie), and after she went in by the dining room
stove to read it, she came running out to the kitchen table where I
was peeling apples for some pies and was just about to cry which
I've never seen that kid do yet. She was trembling all over and she
got her coat and that old hat of Johnnie's she wears all the time.
She said she was going to to the bunkhouse (this was after supper,
Bill) and get Pete to saddle up a horse for her. "Have to go to camp
to see Uncle Shorty," she said, and "This can't wait." She took off,
left the door open, and ran out in the dark towards the bunkhouse.
I thought that child had gone out of her mind, so I grabbed that
long flashlight of yours and took out after her.

Bill, you would have laughed, I did, and later nearly cried too.
Pete's bell mare, Maw, got into too many oats and was sick yesterday (you know, those blamed mules, hee-hawing all morning,
looked scared if a mule can). Pete worked on her half the day and
she got O.K. Then he drove into Roaring River for more horse
medicine, supplies, and the mail. So poor Pete had a hard day.

Well, when I caught up with Sally she was in the dark bunkhouse
pounding on Pete's bed tarp to wake the poor guy up. When I came
in with the flashlight, Pete must have thought the man from Kansas
had shown up again and Sally figured it was him. He was hollering
and the little Shoshone was yelling at him, "Please get up and
saddle a horse for me."

When Pete got his wits about him, he told Sally. "There's only
th' wrangle horse in th' corral besides that sick bell mare, and that
pony is a bronky outfit. Yuh couldn't ride him. It's all I can do to
stay on th' side-winder. Jest a-breakin' him." Pete hunched up in
his tarp bed and rubbed his eyes. "The horses and mules are all
turned out down on 4-mile Meadows. Yuh'll have to wait. I've got
to take the pack string to camp in the morning anyhow, and you
can ride out to see ol' Shorty then."

Sally is on the peck this morning. She's done her hair in a pony
tail, so I know she's mad at somebody.

There was a little more in Vel's letter but it didn't help clear up
the rest of the puzzle I felt a-comin' round the mountain.

Shorty's woodpile looked kinda gant, so Buck Bruen, Al Neeman and me, we got the long cross-cut saw and axes together, and walked over back of camp to cut down some standing dead pine. When I came back to the tent to rummage around for a file, the cook was at the back end of the board table writing furiously and mumbling to himself.

We had four or five good trees down, and were chopping limbs off and sawing the logs into shorter lengths. The wrangler, on the big roan horse, was a-snakin' them over to the woodpile close to the cook tent. One log saw its chance and got an end wedged into a waiting loopy root. Slim was a-whippin' his rope back and forth to drag the log free sidewise, when a big black notebook fell out of his jacket pocket. I was trimming knotty limbs off one down tree close by, so I stepped over, picked it out of a mess of tangled branches and pine chips and handed it up to Slim on his sweaty horse. He reach down, put it into his coat pocket, and buttoned down at me, "If you're curious about the book, it's a diary I put down ideas in." I noticed Al and Buck and listening as Slim went on. "Some day, when I'm old and more harmless, I figure on quittin' this horse jinglin', and I'm goin' to try writing up some stories. The whoppers these locoed guides, the cook, and them hunters tell around these camps is a-goin t' waste. Other damn fools write stories and peddle 'em, maybe there's room for one more."

Buck was sitting on the butt end of a big tree he had just dropped. "I think Slim's got a good idea at that. Here's one for him. A couple days ago Smithers an' me got inta camp kinda early, so Tim went over ta his tent sayin' he was goin' ta take a little snooze. Well, I was over in Slim's bunk and gear tent a-gittin' me a strap ta fix up my knife scabbard." The big guide looked around at the hunters' wall tent over in the edge of the timber, then went on, "Whilst I was a-rummagin' around in there, I heard, right close, a couple uh big *Ka-whoom, Ka-whooms*. I looked out past th' tent flap, and there was that nap-takin' tooth hunter just a-goin' back inta his tent with his cannon still smokin'."

Buck felt of a crack in his axe handle and looked up at the wrangler with a big grin. "I heard some kind of screetchy mumble about that time, an' lookin' over t' th' cook tent, there was ol' Shorty standin' out in front. He was shakin' his fists up and down, an' that flour-sack apron he wears was a-flutterin' in time. Well, I ambled over t' git th' deadwood on this shootin' deal.

"Shorty kinda glares at me, then he says, 'I was a-peelin' these

The wrangler was a-snakin' 'em over to the woodpile.

here spuds an' I happened ta look over inta tha big grassy park that other side of the corral. There was a big mamma coyote a-teachin' her pups how ta catch mice. Them big fluffy pups was pouncin' an' hoppin' in that tall yella grass. An' then all of a sudden that big game hunter starts bombardin' at 'em!' Now you fellas ain't seen nothin' yet, if you never seen Shorty mad."

Bruen carefully looked around at the cook tent. "Then ol' Shorty really gits ta goin'. He says, 'I ain't got enny patience with fellers who's *always* a-tryin' ta kill everything that lives. 'Specially when they don't need 'em t' eat an' they ain't harmin' nobody. Survival of the fittest, Smithers was a-sayin' last night. Why, hell, Buck, many more uh these kind uh leaders uh men, and they'll trail th' whole population right inta purgatory.' "

"Yeah," Al Neeman's a-sittin' on a log over there, filin' on the teeth of the log saw. "Last night I heard Smithers say he came up the hard way, damn hard, he said, an' made a fortune by follerin' his own beliefs. He said he figgered on stickin' with 'em. He says, do onto the other man as he would do onto you, but do it first."

"Well, mebbe he does go by his book," Buck put in to say, "but only a few days ago he saw Pete Elaby showin' me th' gash on his arm where that kickin' mule got him. Tim went 'an got his first-aid kit, a real fancy job, made Pete take his shirt off, an' done as handy a job of dressin' a bad cut as Doc Forrester could of. When he gits done, he says t' Pete, 'O.K., Sucker, you better watch them long-eared politicians. Don't foller 'em, Sucker, lead 'em!' "

Al put in, "Yeah, mebbe he packs a first-aid kit and can use it, but he sure is blind in other ways. He don't seem to *mean* to be vicious to a horse, even if he does put kidney sores on the few he's rode. I showed him one, after I jerked the saddle off his nag last night. He says, 'What th' hell. A horse is only a horse, the poor damn sucker.' "

About that time, a bunch of hee-hawing and wheezy braying down the trail brought Pete Elaby and his packs in sight. We all helped the packer take off his panniers and mantied-up cargo. After dinner, we packed up the quartered meat of Doc Forrester's elk, and his trophy head, on Pete's long-eared partners, and he took off for the ranch, to put the meat in the cooler there.

We spread out for an afternoon hunt in three directions. Parsin got lucky about three miles from camp. I didn't even see him shoot. I was riding up ahead of him, going into a stretch of quaking aspens on an old game trail, the dead fallen branches and leaves making snappy crackles and pops. I thought he was right behind me, when I

A big mamma coyote a-teachin' her pups to catch mice.

heard just one KA-BOOM back in the dark swampy spruce jungle I'd just come out of. I trotted Roany back down the trail; and there, stitting on a very dead glossy big black bear was old Dead-eye George. He said, "I happened to look back down the trail, and there was ol' Fatty following along, dumba as hell." Well, that's hunting, you never know.

After I got back from rounding up that damfool Blackie that George was riding, I tied the two snorting, bear-hating horses close by George's prize. It was pretty dark in there, but George said he was going to take pictures anyhow. I skinned out the bear. When I got through, we decided Slim could pack the meat and hide in the next day. George wanted to take a few movie shots from up on the timbered bench above us, so we rode up there and tied up again.

While he was angling around getting pictures, I was using them high-powered glasses of his looking over the country. Saw a little band of elk, a bull and five cows, grazing high up on Terrace Mountain, partly in the shade of some timber. Suddenly they all spooked at something below them, and took off into the shadows.

Finally I spotted the cause. Those glasses showed two men sitting on the ground close to their tied-up horses, down in a grassy pocket. They'd talk awhile and point around, then get up and walk in and out of sight in the open timber. I finally got the hair focus on these two birds. One of them was a stranger, as far as I could tell. He had a red cloth on his hat and looked like a hunter. The other one, a tall lanky guy, was our horse wrangler. He was only a couple of miles from camp, but it was away off from where we grazed the horse bunch. Just about then, Parsin got his film all used up, so we stepped on our horses and hit for camp. I got to wondering why was Slim pirootin' all over the country. Yesterday Buck told me that while he and Smithers ate lunch a day or so ago on a slope of Terrace Mountain, he was glassing the country with that highfalutin spotting scope of Tim's, he swore he spotted the horse wrangler riding across Nowlin Meadows way down below. Buck was busy trying a new mantle on the gas lantern in the cook tent while he talked. The rest of the gang were out at the meat poles helping Doc Forrester measure his elk head.

"You know, Bill, this Wilson is a good mountain man. Six, eight years ago I was workin' for an outfit on th' other side o' the' mountain. The biggest man in th' crew was an ex-football player. He wouldn't git off th' blazed trail. Nossir, I wouldn't a believed it either, until his hunter beefed about it. If he couldn't find a nich-an'-a-slash ranger blaze on a tree, he wouldn't go. 'A game trail is a snare an' a delusion,'

The other guy was our horse wrangler.

he said. 'Damn elk especially, tryin' t' foul yuh up, every time.' Yuh kin sure git some queer ones. Th' boss of this outfit said he hired a cowboy once, fer guide. Good man with horses, go anywhere, up, down, through th' worst jungle y' ever seen; or try it. The hell of it was, this bird would never git off his horse. No sir, he wouldn't. Eat, sleep, help good around camp, split wood 'n' help wrangle. But he wouldn't walk a hunderd yards. Once he had them legs clamped around a horse, he was set till he got back t' camp. So th' boss tried it different next year, he said. He put an ad in th' paper, which read: 'Wanted—Experienced Guide and Packer. Cowboy will do, if willing to learn.' Out of five he tried out that year, four were cowboys, but three of 'em made th' grade. Their legs an' dome hadn't been warped too bad, an' they never took th' movies an' Will James too serious. No shadow riders. Slim, he's no shadow rider, either. Mebbe he's a mystery, but he shore is a good hand."

This traveling wrangler sure done all the horse work O.K., helped with the wood, and packed in all the game the hunters killed, so I had no kick. But he had an uncanny way of getting around in a bunch of mountains strange to him. He sure was a mountain man, anyhow. Shorty mentioned a time or two that Slim often didn't show up for dinner, and all Slim packed for a gun was a battered old .38 six-shooter.

George and I got back to camp early, and all we found there was a crummy old porcupine trying to rustle his way into the gear tent. He hadn't made the grade, so we run him off. George got his fishing gear and went over to the river to try for trout. I got some chores done around camp. It began to get dark, and no cook yet, so I started up the fires—Shorty's stove in the cook tent, the Dutch oven fire outside, and the stove in the hunters' tent. Just as I shut that one down, I thought I heard two quick rifle shots somewhere in the heavy timber above camp.

Wilson and Shorty Beel always had got along fine. They seemed to be friends from the time we brought Slim out with us. But I'd noticed lately a peculiar coolness in their attitude towards each other. Was it just since Smithers started up his talk about collecting elk teeth?

This here Terrace Mountain had some copper veins. An outfit had put in two, three years exploring, digging shafts, looking for the mother lode. Had a big camp once, just below where our camp sets. An old fell-down cabin or two around here yet. Mebbe one of these two birds had hit it rich, and figured the other was a claim jumper. The cook had guided and packed over this country for years, before arthritis had bent up his carcass. He knew the whole country like the back of his hand. The horse jingler had been around these parts maybe a couple weeks. Sometimes a newcomer finds things an old-timer has seen for years and didn't see for what it was. Or had he?

I tied up the tent flaps and stood outside listening for any more shots, when the horse bells started up their music, and soon Slim was driving the bunch into the corral. I called when he was putting the poles in the gate, "Didja hear a coupla shots up on th' mountain, just now, Slim?"

"Sure, Bill, but them horses had me busy an' I couldn't tell where from. Al and Buck and their hunters went down th' Buffalo to hunt, so it couldn't a been them." The wrangler gave a quick look up Terrace Mountain. "After all you fellows left this afternoon, Shorty told me he was a-goin' to walk up that steep draw back of camp. He said, he thinks Terrace Mountain might have some uranium, and he could use a few shekels." Slim grinned. "I was tackin' a shoe on the buckskin when he left, so I don't know whether he packed a gun or not. Mebbe elk teeth are surer'n uranium, haw, haw."

"That remind me, Slim," I said, trying to catch him, "I spotted you on Terrace three or four hours ago with Parsin's glasses. Looked like somebody was with you."

Slim never batted an eye. "I sure was up there." He had a big grin. "I thought I'd look at the formation, too. Horses O.K. down here. I met a hunter from a camp on Sody Fork across the ridge. He hadn't shot an elk, he said, but I learned a lot about the country from him."

The wrangler went on up to the gear tent and came back with a sack of oats, so I helped him grain the horses. About then George Parsin came through the timber with a string of big trout. "I got enough for supper, with that liver Smithers is sure to bring in. Maybe those two shots awhile ago mean Tim got a bull with two more teeth."

The Dutch ovens were on the hot coals, and I had started to cook, when Shorty showed up in the dark, outside the tent. He looked sour and grumpy, but says, "Thanks, Bill. I'll take over now." He didn't even ask who got the trout that I'd rolled in cornmeal and had ready for the Dutch oven. About then Buck Bruen and Smithers rode in. "Tim got a big bull three hours or so ago, down below Bear Cub Pass," Buck said. "Good big rack and two big teeth. All he needs now is nine hundred and ninety-six more, haw, haw."

Al Neeman and Doc Forrester rode in right after that, and Doc untied a big deer liver from the back of his saddle. "Hey, Shorty," he hollered, "More meat for the pan." Shorty didn't even look up from the Dutch oven, just waved his pot hook and grunted in Doc

Forrester's direction. He pried up the Dutch oven lid to take a peek at how the trout were doing, and Smithers got a whiff of the real thing. "If I could cook like you can, Shorty, I'd have the best restaurants in New York." "Yeah," Shorty grunted at him, and looked out at the still night, "Sure windy tonight, ain't it?"

We all just got set down to eat, when we *could* hear a big wind come up all of a sudden. Doc Forrester was telling about killing his buck deer down in the vee west of Terrace Mountain, and was waving his fork with a piece of fried liver on its business end, in his description of the running deer. We could hear the timber tops moan and whistle, up back of camp. The wind interrupted Doc, whipping up the loose cook tent flaps with a tearing pop, then something plenty heavy smacked down on the tent pole. The chimney wires whangled, and down comes a pipe section. Smoke, sparks, and powdery soot came pouring out of the stove, choking and blinding the whole crew. We all got up and ran outside in the dark, in a tangled mess of arms and legs.

Tim Smithers was last, being clear in the back of the cook tent. He was on his way, when the gas lamp shimmied off the wire wrapped to the shaking tent pole. The lamp fell smack dab into a platter full of French-fried spuds, and sizzled out. The big-footed hunter got tangled in the bail of a Dutch oven. He fell flat, his high-priced nose buried in a pile of piping hot liver and onions. Old Shorty, first out, was hollering real frantic, "Look out fer my sourdough keg, yuh damn fools!" By that time he got his flashlight going. When we got the liver-cured millionaire and the hot stove pacified, we found it *wasn't* a crazy grizzly, it was a big dead flowzy branch that had busted out of a all tree quite a ways off. It musta come pinwheeling down in the wind dead center for our tent.

We finally got the sections of stovepipe wired back, and the liver and onions off of Tim's face and ears. Buck started the gas lamp up. Al and I were a-cleaning the soot off the table boards. The genial doctor from Indiana and George Parsin were washing some tin dishes and kidding Shorty, who was a little happier, having found his keg as safe as ever. We were ready to eat again.

We just got set down to have at it, when Smithers, in a clean shirt, showed up in the tent door. He looked all around with a greasy smirk, pulled a hand out from behind him, and held up a big piece of fried liver. "To the victor belong the spoils, suckers."

Chapter Eight

The next morning George Parsin had a bad attack of rheumatism, so Doctor Forrester wanted to stay in camp and doctor up George with a few rub-downs he was sure would help. Buck and Al Neeman helped Slim tighten up and re-shoe a few of the saddle horses during the doctoring. Smithers said he'd like to hunt up around Nowlin Mountain again, so he and I took off. Besides, we decided to look at the bear bait, an old worn-out pack horse we'd planted a week or so before, in a timber surrounded park close to Line Creek.

After he missed the bear, Smithers had dirty looks for anybody who mentioned how handy a flashlight was. Early in the evening we tied our horses in the timber a hundred yeards or so from the dead horse, and made a sneak through the trees to where we could see the bait. Sure enough, it was ripe enough to have a visitor. On the opposite side of the carcass, we could see the big black. Standing upright, he'd stoop over from the hips, to gnaw and tear at the paunch of the old sorrel pony. Then he'd straigthen up bloody nose snuffling and paws dangling, to look over at the timber diagonal to us. His chompy growls in that direction looked like he figured company was coming. About half of that timber surrounded park was in the sunlight. The long shadows, cast by the spruce timber we hid in, reached out just to touch the carcass.

A small breeze sprang up, rippling the tall yellow grass, and bringing the perfume straight from the dining room. It didn't seem to bother the broker. At a nod from me, he started to raise his rifle. I held my nose to keep down a cough, while I watched his finger take up the slack on the trigger. Just as Smithers shot, the bear jumped over the horse and tore off, coughing and snarling at something over to our left. "Why, that lucky dam sucker!" Smithers jammed the butt of his rifle on the ground, and started to cuss.

While we walked back to the horses, I tried to console that mad hunter. "Hell, Tim, that bear didn't even know you shot. He was chasin' some other bear off. We can come here early in th' mornin' and you can git another shot at th' same bear, I'll betcha."

By the time we walked around a small swamp to within sight of

82

our horses, I forgot about bear and done a little cussin' of my own. There was only one horse in sight and he looked mighty lonesome. "Any horse-thieves in these parts, Bill?" was Smithers' comment as we walked up to my horse. "Nope, I don't reckon so; but a big Boy Scout from New York" (I see Smithers starin' bug-eyed at where he'd tied his horse) "is plumb afoot, bear or no bear." Tim always insisted he was able to handle his own horse, so he felt flabbergasted to see nothing but the wrong end of the neckrope tied to the tree. Also, a long-handled flashlight was lying on the ground where it had fallen from the saddlebag of his departed horse. "My bowline musta slipped," he says, fingering the rope, "but we can see, if it gets dark. Good thing the horse left the flashlight." From the sign and tracks I found, I figgered our bear, or maybe two, had come this way and scared the horses. I cast around, making circles, trying to find which way the stray horse went before it got dark.

Finally I told Smithers to ride my horse back to camp, about two miles. I'd walk up to a high grassy park, just above us a hundred yards or so, get the lost horse, and ride him into camp. "I know old Prunes drifted up there," I told Smithers. "That's an old campsite of ours. His tracks head that way anyhow." I saw Smithers ride off packing his flashlight under one arm, down toward the ranger trail that led to camp. He'd put his rifle in my scabbard, and I carried mine as I climbed up the hill.

Well, I found Prunes right in the old pole corral. He was licking at a small lump of salt and looked plumb at home. It was plenty dark when I rode up to the corral at camp. I expected to hear Smithers haw-hawing up at Shorty's cook tent. I could hear all the others talking, and see the shadows they made around the table, but no Tim. I tied Prunes up to a corral pole, with the horses inside nosing at him for the news. As I walked over towards the cook tent a horse nickered in the trail. Turned out to be my horse, that Smithers had rode off. I was looking Roany over in the dark, when Wilson opened the tent flap and came over to where I was.

"Hi, Bill, where's Tim?"

When I told Slim about the bear and about when I last saw Smithers and his flashlight, he started to laugh. By that time, Buck, Al, Shorty, and the two hunters came out of the cook tent to hear the palaver. We found Smithers' rifle in the scabbard under the left stirrup leather of my saddle. Outside of the absence of the broker and his flashlight everything was O.K.; Roany himself acted plumb spooky. You know, that dang Wilson is a sharpie. When he started to *laugh*, it kinda got my dander up. But Slim musta seen several flashlights and horses in his time.

The boys saddled up horses, and I got up on Roany, leading Prunes. We trotted back up the trail, wondering if we'd find shreds of stocks and bonds clear to the upper canyon. That roan sure acted real spooky. I wondered what he'd done to Tim. We rode a mile or so up the trail, dark as the inside of a tar barrel, when there come a big circle of light and a loud holler, and there was Wilson in the light, imitating Booger Red coming outa chute number three. Wilson was riding the freshest horse and was in the lead; if he hadn't been plumb forked he'd a lit in the rocks. By the time Slim got his horse under control, we found Smithers in the trail mumbling, "Why, that tough dam sucker, why, that tough dam sucker!" And that danged money bags was still waving that blamed flashlight around.

All the broker would say, when we asked him how come, was, "Got tired of riding that dam sucker." By the time we got back to camp and had shoveled in some of the cook's good food, Smithers was in a better mood. He got around to noticing the puzzled grins, and finally come out with it. "If you birds want to get a good education, just show one of these western horses the Great White Way." He started to rub his knees. "I thought Roany had lost the trail, so I snapped on my flashlight to show him the way to go home. He put me right where the beam lit."

We got a real early start next morning. Buck, with Tim, and Al, with Doc, went off toward Pendergraf Meadows; but George Parsin had a moose permit, and I thought I knew where a big bull hung out; so we were touring across the river in the spruce jungle, cut up with willow bogs and swamps, looking for a big-nosed gent with panned horns. When we got up on a knobby ridge, down there feeding in a floating bog was old record-buster himself, him and two floppy-snouted lady friends. George whispers real quiet-like, "I'm a-going to lower the boom on that gent." We were in the shadows of some big spruce trees and were off our horses. The pleased hunter got his gun laid across a down log, and was getting set to aim at the unsuspecting bull, when a dead quaking aspen tree decided to liven up the proceedings. Just a busted-up second before George could shoot, this tree gave up its shallow-rooted ghost, and fell, KA-WHOUNCHY-BANG, right in between poor old George and the three swamp lovers. Them three moose had plumb evaporated when George got through swearing.

As the moose hadn't seen us, and was used to the tricks trees play in the mountains, we went after them. We were riding real cagey-like, with stops and starts, through that messy pothole country, and hadn't got sight of our quarry yet, when we came up on a spiny open ridge. We stopped to take our bearings. I got off my horse, and was using George's fine binoculars again. I happened to swing them past old Tinsley's mine shaft hole up on the side of an open draw a quarter of a mile away. Dang my wrinkled-up old hide, if I didn't spot the cook, old Shorty; he had a sack on his back, and was just about to enter that black hole on the steep sidehill. I held the glasses on Shorty till he disappeared. I moved them a little, and then spotted a movement on a timbered point two or three hundred yards above the long-abandoned copper dream of old man Tinsley.

Hell, no, it wasn't that big bull moose that George Parsin had his soul set on. It was Big Slim the horse wrangler. Why, dang my miserable wrinkled-up hide all over again.

Parsin was sitting impatiently on his horse. He whispered a real anxious Jim Bridger whisper, "Do you see any sign of our friends yet, Bill?" I gave a fool grunty "Not yet," because up there was the horse jingler sitting behind a log; with a long telescope trained right down on old Shorty's hidey-hole. And right now he wasn't my friend.

I figger I'd better get my mind on normal moose instead of crazy men, so I told George we'd probably better make a big circle up around the blown-down timber we'd got into, and hit them beaver pond pockets just below the ridge. Well, we did, finally, and after about two hours of hard traveling, I'll be dad-burned if we didn't see old Pappy Big-nose himself, with his two snooty girl friends, and he didn't have any jittery trees to help him this time. He seen us, too, and blustered up into a mud-slinging trot right out of a beaver pond. He had a water-lily root in his dripping schnozzle, but that didn't camouflage him a bit. He was in a big splashy hurry, but my hunter was faster. The old willow-cruncher fell just on the slippery bank of the boggy pond, but his discreet lady friends didn't wait for the ceremony.

While I cleaned out the moose, the happy hunter took a lot of pictures. When I got through, George helped me turn the huge carcass over on some limbs to cool out. After that, we cut and piled green branches on the roan hide of the old monarch of the timbered jungle. It looked like snow was coming, and we probably wouldn't pack the old boy in to camp till next day.

All this time I'd forgotten about that scene played by Shorty and the horse wrangler. But now, old Doc's idea of a mountain ulcer

I held the glasses on Shorty.

started gnawing at my innards again. I thought Shorty was the wrong kind of mouse if Slim was paying cat. Mebbe Slim *was* going to write stories someday. If so, he sure was getting plots, but this one had me stumped.

It was a big surprise when we got into camp, early in the afternoon, to find the whole gang there, except the horse wrangler; and I soon saw him on the bench across the river, rounding up the horses to bring to the corral. The cook was bustling around, banging pots and pans. He was even grinning at Tim Smithers' big haw-haw cracks about Shorty's "square-rumped gait." Al Neeman told me "The Big Haw-haw" bagged a buck deer on the way back to camp—that was why he felt so jovial. "Too bad bucks don't have tusks, ain't it, Tim?" came from Shorty this time. Smithers puts out another of his so-called quips: "A tooth for a tooth," he says, "I'll trade anybody all my buck teeth for just one elk tusk." When the whole gang started haw-hawing, he saw his crack had backfired: that big freckled mug of his had a whole mouthful of buck teeth. He musta got mad then; anyhow, he flushed up and grunted, "To hell with you suckers," and stalked over to his tent.

Just before supper, George Parsin borrowed a needle and thread from Shorty, to patch his jacket, and mentioned how he'd got snagged by some tree limbs he'd rode under. "You sure don't dare to go to sleep riding through the timber. I thought I was low enough to clear that limb." That started talk about how much wear and tear clothes take to survive. The cook laughed, "when I was younger, I used to buy guaranteed britches; 'ten cents a button, a dollar a rip,' that's what th' label read." Buck said, "You ain't as old as I thought you was, Shorty. I used t'wear that brand, too. Can't buy that kind any more. They don't make 'em."

Shorty put the grub on the table, and we all started to eat. Buck went on talking: "Damfool things happen, to clothes and people, too. By hell, you'd a thought, as much as I've rammed around in th' hills, it would never a happened to me. We was huntin' moose, an' was headed for them willow bottoms on Soda Fork. My hunter an' me had just rode outa some heavy timber onta a grassy hog back. Then we started ridin' down a steep game trail slanted down a gravelly hillside. My hunter was comin' along about thirty feet behind me. When he whistled, I looked back an' up ta where he pointed, an' saw a big ol' osprey a-glarin' down from a snaggy limb on th' top of a tall dead pine. I waved, 'Come on,' an' turned back, jist in time t' have a small dead tree fall over on my saddle, between me an' th' horn. It knocked th' reins outa my hand, then that damfool horse spooked an' ran between two trees an' hung up. My knees were too wide f'r th' doorway, an' that ever-lovin' tree had me by th' chin. Yessir, I was dang near chokin' t' death, spread out on the horse's back, when th' hunter rode around an' grabbed my horse's head." Buck grinned and rubbed his belly. "Any you birds wanta see th' scars them branches made? My hunter called me 'Fish Hawk' th' rest a that trip. And, y' know, them pants still held together."

After this early supper, here come another puzzle. I hadn't heard it for days, but Wilson was humming a little tune, as he put the horse bunch out. . . . And a while later, the two guides and I were over in the trees, looking at the game carcasses hung on the meat poles back of the tents. We could hear Doctor Forrester and George comparing notes on the day's hunts. Hearing some large haw-haws in another direction, I looked over; and back of the cook tent, there was Shorty listening to Smithers, and derned if he wasn't nodding his head and grinning as that big beefy millionaire waved his hands around. Tim's loud voice sure carried, but the only words I heard plain were: "Can I depend on this, Shorty? It'll be cash every time, and I don't mean maybe." The cook grinned and nodded his head, and it looked like they shook hands. Why, damn it all, them belly wobblers of mine started up again.

The hunt was about over, but that was the one I'll never forget if I live to be 100. As Smithers started to walk over to his tent, I happened to think of his yen for a bear hide, so I sang out, "Oh, Tim, how about us takin' a look at th' bear bait? We'll still have shootin' light. This is your last chance if you're goin' in, in the mornin'." "Thanks, Bill," Smithers still had a big grin on is mug, "I think I'll pass it up. No bear's going to make a sucker outa me twice!"

For some fool reason, the cook and the horse wrangler, who'd been good friends the first part of this hunt, had in the last few days been as distant and suspicious of each other as two turpentined strange bobcats. But as we started to gab around the table this evening, Shorty pouring coffee all around, I noticed he and Slim were burying the hatchet. Wilson was cracking jokes at Shorty; and the cook, looking puzzled, was meeting the friendly cracks with some salty comments of his own. Al and Buck were staring at them, too, with odd grins at their horsey humor; here were these two porkypines about to be lovebirds. I thought about mine shaft holes, lost horses, shots in the night, the wandering horse wrangler, and the deal behind the cook tent. Was there a Smithers in the woodpile?

Well, Pete Elaby got into camp next morning with his jacks, and he brought some mail. We were going to eat dinner, and then pack all the hunters' meat and trophies and their camp gear on Pete's mules and some of our pack horses. Their hunt was over, and they were going on in to the ranch and then home. I spotted a letter for me from Velma, so I went over to the woodpile and sat down in the sun to read it. I noticed the rest of the crowd had mail except Slim Wilson. He was helping Shorty set the table, and joking about something.

Velma's letter was good; it read, among other things; "Bill, you'll be interested in a note from Warren Kompton. Sally and I were, to say the least." I found the note, and it *was* interesting.

"Dear Bill, Hope your hunting camp is operating O.K. Regards to the crew and hunters. When I got back to Roaring River, I couldn't find hide nor hair of your friend from Kansas. But a couple days ago a warden stopped in. He told me that the law down at the county seat had a hunter from Kansas in jail there. Seems like this gent got more than fresh with a lady he somehow mistook for a wayward waitress. Evidently he had a snootful at the time. The lady turned out to be the mayor's wife. Anyhow, there he is. Story is, he refused to use any *dumb, local lawyer* for defense. He said the governor of Kansas will raise hell with the *hillbilly mayor* for this outrage. Yours, the Game Warden."

After that, I felt pretty good, and hungry. We ate Shorty's fine dinner, and soon the hunters were all set to go with the pack string to the ranch; they'd all settled up their bills with me, and they and the rest of us were visiting around for the last time.

Then I noticed the cook, off to one side, halfway hidden by the cook tent, talking alone with Smithers. They seemed kind of furtive, and it looked like Smithers was buttoning a package into a large pocket of his heavy hunting coat. I saw him handing Shorty a handful of bills, which the cook carefully counted. Old Money-bags watched Shorty, then he started hee-hawing. "I'll sure be looking for the rest of 'em," he said. Pete Elaby and Slim were throwing a diamond hitch on the last jack loaded with the hunters' gear, and Slim was watching the cook and Smithers over the mule's back. Damned if *he* didn't have a sly grin on *his* face under that big hat. I wondered if *all* the wolves had gone to the big cities.

The wrangler was going to help Pete take the pack string in to the ranch, and was going to come back with the pack horses. Just before the hunters got on their horses, we shook hands all around. Doc Forrester and George Parsin planned on a hunt with us next fall, and said they'd write. The big hunter, Tim Smithers, said, "I don't think

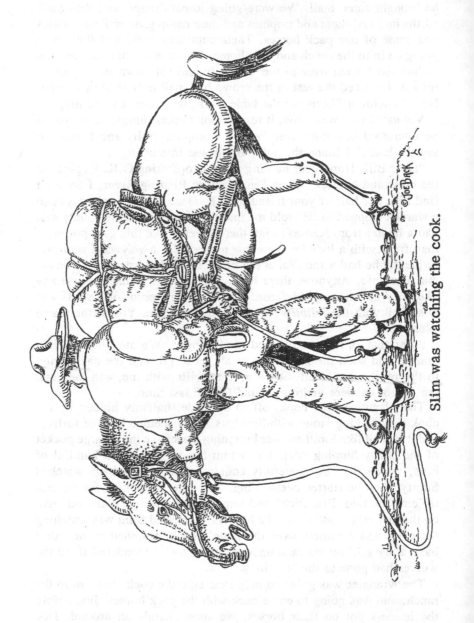

Slim was watching the cook.

I'll be out. I'll have what I want out of these mountains by Christmas."
He grins a big toothy grin. "If any of you birds need any good stocks
or bonds, just write old Timothy Smithers and Co." As they disappeared down the trail, that big voice boomed out of the timber, "So
long, suckers, haw, haw, haw!"

Shorty was hanging some wet towels he'd just washed on a tent
rope, as I came over. He was mumbling to himself, so I says, "I didn't
git that, what didja say, Shorty?" He hung another towel on the rope,
and looked at me kinda grouchy-like. "I said, that trail Smithers is
a-follerin' ain't a straight one. Many a long, smooth trail has a lotta
big slide rock at the other end."

Now that we had the hunters off our hands, us four fellers decided
to get our own elk for our winter meat. We had only a few days till
hunting season was over. I told the other boys they could hunt where
they pleased, but I was going to hunt across the Buffalo Fork till
evening. I saddled up the big roan and took off.

When I got across the river, I rode up on a timbered point where I
could see camp. Al Neeman and Buck were a-ridin' off up the trail
towards the falls, and the cook was busy taking down the hunters'
tent, so I knew I could do what snooping I had on my mind without
getting caught at it.

Finally Roany got the hill climbed and I got off and tied him up in
the shadow of the heavy timber, just above Tinsley's shaft hole on
the steep sidehill. I knew where Slim was, and I was dern sure Shorty
wouldn't have time to git up here, as I slid and stumbled down into
the pile of rocks and rotted timbers at the entrance of the long-faded
dream of a copper empire.

Looked safe enough, so I went in. There was a hole for about twenty
feet. Beyond was just a pile of shattered greenish rock all fallen
together. A huge pile of sticks, old rotten pieces of moldy canvas,
leaves, pine needles, fuzzy remnants of hair and grass, along with a
bitter acrid stink—all this showed that here was the high-class mansion
of some industrious pack rats. That's all I could see at first. Sun was
in the wrong direction. I lit some matches. All I found was some odd
sprinklings of a slick white odorless powder, a lot of candle ends
burned clear to smears, a couple poles laid side by side, with four-five
old gunny sacks on top of the poles, and a couple empty bottles. They
smelled something like hack-sor-been liniment. I dug around in the
mess of pack rat nests, ran out of matches, and gave up. A hell of a
Sherlock on horseback, I was.

Roany was fidgeting around, snorting at nothing, I thought. He had wound around the tree he was tied to, so his neck rope was tight. I was winded from that climb up from the mine hole. After I'd got him unwound and got on him, I found the cause. A band of elk were bedded in the heavy timber right behind him and he tried to tell me; but by the time I got my rifle unlimbered they'd got away. It was getting dark by then, so I turned him downhill and headed for camp.

When I got close to camp, I saw old Shorty's shadow moving inside the lighted-up cook tent. It was getting colder'n hell, and he had the tent flaps down, but I could hear that old Bill Rema stove a-panting. The boys hadn't got in yet, so I unsaddled and got some oats from the gear tent. I was graining the horse bunch Slim had left in the corral, when Buck and Al rode in and got off their ponies to help.

Well, we put the bells on the bell horses and they throwed the bunch over on the big bench and anchored their picket horses to a couple logs. By that time it was plumb dark and Shorty was hollering, "Grub's on, come an' git it," so we rambled over to the cook tent.

Old Shorty was humping around the table, filling our tin plates full of that good grub of his; then he sat down himself, to start in. Al and Buck had got lucky. They had both got a cow apiece, after running into some, skirmishing around in the quaking aspens long Line Creek, above the falls. They were going to pack'em into camp in the morning. I finally got the talk see-sawed around to the old copper mine that was just below camp—the whys and wherefores of the mother lode, sudden fortune, frustrated hopes, and hard work for nothing. Had it going strong, and was about to get the talk wrangled around to Tinsley's dream of a copper fortune, when the cook blew my Sherlock Holmes idea all to hell.

"You birds know that old shaft up th' draw across th' river? Well, that old hole, that Tinsley spent a year or so diggin', is youranium 'stead of copper. I ain't got no reglar Gigglin' counter, but my arthuritis has got that beat. No matter what you wise birds say, every time I'm a-travelin', afoot or a-horseback, I know when I'm over rich youranium country. If my joints gits ta feelin' O.K. all of a sudden, then I know I'm over rich stuff. All I gotta do then is ta move so far thisaway or thataway, and when she gits to givin' me hell again, then I know I'm past th' lode.

"Now, you smart gents think yore a-goin' ta git rich a-guidin' people like ol' Elk Tooth Smithers all over these hills. Now, me, I ain' a-goin' ta have ta rob no poor widders an' orphans t' git mine. I've tromped 'n' rode over these same mountains a-doin' th' same thing you're a-doin' a long time before you gents was weaned. I've got areas mapped out, with my built-in Gigglin' counter, in places you fellers wouldn't dream of. I know you boys won't try ta jump my claim up in that hole. But I'll give yuh each a share as witnesses."

The cook has got all steamed up now. William J. Bryant woulda had his jaw fractured on his own briskit-top to have heard Shorty's oration.

"You fellers probly wondered where'n hell I was a-wanderin' off ta when you was a-huntin'." Shorty had done forgot to eat his own vittles now, he's goin' so strong. "Well, youranium's a hell of a good cure for arthuritis, as I was a-sayin'. Pervided yuh c'n stand th' strain of th' pain a-leavin' yuh sudden-like. I go up ta Tinsley's lost hope hole, rub my liniment an' medicine powder around on my joints, an' lay down on some poles I got up there. Bin a-doin' it ever chance I git, between cookin' fer dude hunters an' damfool guides. Feel a damn sight better'n I have fer years. Mebbe I c'n git 'nough grub up there, an' stay all winter. I gotta notion ta try it."

That wrinkled-up squinty blue-eyed cook had us breath-bound with his story. But when we got our wind back we couldn't hold it. Shorty acted sore as hell at our haw-haws. If he ain't a hillbilly Barrymore he sure as hell means what he says. I got dizzy about then. That package I'd seen Smithers button up in a coat pocket. That roll of bills that'd choke a moose. That haw-haw hand-wavin'. That "Can I depend on that?" and, "It'll be cash every time, Shorty." Hell, yes, I got it now. Must be!

Old Full-pockets is grub-stakin' Shorty. He's taking rich uranium samples back with him. Old Stocks-and-bonds is going to get more samples of uranium, and big Smithers Uranium Corporation is a-going to beat some more widders and orphans. Is Shorty turning crooked or is he being took? That elk tooth business is just my own hell-lucy-na-tion. Boy, my belly-wobbling settled down now. And, man, did I eat Shorty's good cooking?

What with one thing and another happening, Shorty and me, we got our elk, too. The wrangler and Pete Elaby came in from the ranch with their pack string in a day or so. By that time, we had everything ready to go. By noon we had the whole camp, meat and all, packed in to the ranch. The snow started to fall just as we pulled in.

Vel had the corral gate open for us. Her eyes were sparkling, and she was just a-bustin' with something she wanted to tell.

"You throw off the packs and hurry up to the house, she says, real sassy. "Dinner's all ready, and you want to hear the latest about the man from Kansas!"

Chapter Nine

Turned out to be quite a tale Vel told while we ate.

"Yesterday, I went to town, mostly to see if my sister Minnie was over her sick spell. She was entertaining the 'Top of the Mountain Club' and looked as healthy as any of Pete's mules." Velma had a bad case of giggles.

During the luncheon with this group of Roaring River's housewives and ranch-women, she heard the man from Kansas' name mentioned, she said.

It seemed that Bessie Brumley, the veteran nurse at Roaring River's doctor's office, observed that very peculiar wounds seemed to pop up among hunters during hunting season. According to Velma, Bessie went on to say, "This bird showed up in the waiting room, banging the door and mumbling to himself. The place was plumb full of people, most of 'em with appointments, some of these really needing the doctor's help. Well, when I told this man to write his name and address down on the pad and sit down to wait his turn, he got real uppity. I didn't cotton to this gent atall, looked like a heavy drinker and a big eater. See 'em alla time. All alike, too. Big bay window and back porch to match, plus that boiled beak, all gave him away.

"Well, girls, you see'em all th' time! Figured he had a hangover and needed an aspirin.

"I thought I'd humor him, so, real sweet, I told this character, 'Well, Mister, if it is urgent and you are a-hurtin' real bad, tell me what's it about, and I'll get word to the doctor. He's setting a kid's broken leg right now.' Well, girls, you'da laughed, too, if you'd a seen this guy then. He swelled up like a pouter pigeon, glared around at the other patients waiting in the chairs around the room, glared at me, and then leaned up close to the counter I was behind; and then he started to unwind a long and fancy muffler he had twisted around his neck. I could see some scratchy cuts on top of his ears and underneath 'em. He also had some fuzzy cuts on his chin, and a little cotton pad was stuck up on a singed place on his bushy hair.

"When I saw that, and those little pig eyes a-glarin' at me, I remembered the badger that got caught in old Harley Dedrick's chicken house on the ranch. The hen's private door was a little too small and the

94

badger too big. I couldn't help but think this bird must have something in common with the badger, so I just had to laugh, even if he didn't have any feathers in his mouth.

"That tore it. This gent whipped the muffler around his neck and stomped out, snarling something about hill-billy pill peddlers and their no-good help."

The crew had a big laugh over this news about Kansas, and Pete says, "That's our boy, but how in thunder did he git them cuts?"

Vel had another giggle for this. "I'm saving that story for you, too." She went on, "While Bessie was telling about Kansas and his cuts, Pauline Bucknem started to laugh, and she told the interested ladies that she had the answer to that one."

Seemed like the day before Bessie had the encounter with the hunter in Doctor Mack's office, the six-year-old son of Pauline's had a cold, so she let him stay home from school. She hadn't told Willy, her husband, about it, as he started out to his welding shop in front of their house. "Willie's Welding" was known for miles around the mountains as the best in the business, and he was always busy.

The boy with the cold looked out the window when he heard the loud blaring of a car horn. From his bed on the couch he could just see the front end of a big car peeking past the shop building's front door.

His curiosity hurt him more than his throat did, when he saw a bare-headed man with a wide white collar going into his dad's shop. Just as soon as he made sure that his mother, in the kitchen, was washing dishes with her hands and reading a who-dun-it with her eyes, he felt safe enough to ease out the front door. Sometimes his favorite knot hole was obscured by some piece of machinery leaned up inside the busy place, but this time he could see nearly the whole shop's inside. Billy could see the barrel-shaped man waving his hands and taking to Willie. The breathless boy saw his dad nodding his head and taking a bill from the man. Then he heard Willie say, "Sure, Mister, I won't tell a soul. The price is right, but it'll be a ticklish job."

Billy looked over towards the house and sw that he was still safe. He stuck his runny nose up against the rough board, and glued his eye back to the hole; this was worth any strapping his dad could give him. He noticed the long hunting knife strapped to the straining belt, and decided this hunter was different, this one must have a bad cold and his collar was hurting. After he saw his grinning father break several hack saw blades on the collar, Billy suddenly realized that the collar was a *white-enameled toilet seat*. His dad finally had to resort to the cutting torch before the collar gave up. Billy decided he'd seen enough. He barely made it to the couch, before his mother came in from the kitchen to see about her ailing scholar.

Pauline told the ladies that Willy, during meals or at odd times while in the house, would break into fits of sudden laughter, then clam up. She took to watching him, as welding is a chancy life; but Billy, sensing the undertow, told his mother all about it. Pauline finally got Willy to squeal.

"Well," Velma ended, "of course, I had to tell them the rest. The poor guy—that's all the use he ever got out of that toilet seat."

Slim commented, poker faced, "He got more mileage out of his than most men expect to."

"So much for Kansas," says I, getting up, "She's snowing pretty hard, and we got lots to do."

Pete, Buck, and Al were going to help me put up some cabins. But Slim said he was going down to the lower country for the winter. So I settled up with him, and told him that if he ever wanted a job with my kind of outfit, just to holler, for I could use an A-1 hand any time. He said, "Bill, it's been a pleasure to work for you. I've learned a lot about the country, and some new things about people. If there is a finer bunch of fellers to work with, I ain't seen 'em. I'll drop you a line soon to ask how you boys are stackin' up." He shook hands all around, and threw his saddle, bed roll, and war bag in the pickup. Pete Elaby had to go to town and was taking him in. As they went down the road and through the trees, I was thinking of the warm way Slim Wilson had shook hands with old Shorty. The cook was grinning, and sorry to see Slim leave. The riddle was Slim's last remark to the cook, "So long, old-timer, take care o' yourself, and don't let them elk teeth get mixed up with that uranium." Then I saw Shorty, his face all squinted up in a puzzled frown, leaning against the kitchen door. He watched the old green pickup disappearing through the falling snow, till it faded out of sight in the timber.

Well, here it goes again; why didn't I tell Pete to bring back some more Rocky Mountain ulcer pills?

Shorty Beel, the cook, had a few acres close to town. A lot of the little town was built on land Shorty had sold from his homestead to late settlers. He rebuilt guns, saddles, and pack outfit gear, and was a clever tinker with a lot of things. He was an industrious and thrifty old mountain man. When my wife and I would go to town, sometimes we'd stay over with this old friend for a few days. Come holidays, the old boy would stay with us.

The only person closer to Shorty was his nephew, who was now pretty close to being a full-fledged dentist. He was in school in the same big town Smithers called his. Old Shorty planned to stay at the ranch a few days to rest up; but right after Slim pulled out, the cook get restless and said he had to go home. There was some things he wanted to fix up and send to Johnny in New York. He says, kinda worried-like, "I shoulda went in with Pete an' Slim. I plumb fergot about that stuff fer Johnny."

This sudden yen to get to town had me up a stump. It didn't help the stump any, even when here comes the pickup back, with Pete and Slim a-grinning in the cab. Pete had forgot the chains, and that snow was getting deep and slippery. While Pete went over to the shop for the tire chains, Slim and I helped Shorty get all his gear and them big private panniers into the back of the truck. After seeing him get in between Pete and Slim, I said so long again to Slim and told Shorty I'd drop in for a visit soon. Away they went the second time. Pete was sure making good time. The clackety-clack chain end hitting the fender was real noisy. I figured, by the jumped-up Judas, I oughta feel better now, getting rid of two ulcers at the same time.

Chapter Ten

During all the flurry of unpacking the mules and horses; stacking panniers, tents, stoves, and the rest of the camp gear; taking care of our meat; eating dinner; and now all this goodbyeing, I'd forgotten to ask what happened to Sally. We expected to find her at the ranch with Velma, but she was gone.

"You know, Bill, that girl was sure changed when she came back with Pete from camp, after she saw Shorty." Vel was unpacking some kitchen panniers, and putting left-over camp food supplies into the store room off the kitchen. "I had to slow her up. She jumped into the ranch work with such vim, I thought she'd have a nervous breakdown. I really got worried about her. She lost that sunny disposition, and several times I saw her stop and stare at nothing, like she was in a trance. She wouldn't tell me anything. All I could get out of that kid was mumbles about 'sneaky city slickers.' Then, the day before the hunters came in to the ranch from camp, Sally had a phone call from Tom Hoster, her brother-in-law down on the reservation. He was calling from his ranch to tell Sally that her sister was very sick and it was serious. . . . Yes, Pete took her home in the pickup. He said she hardly said a word during the trip. That packer sure is a driver, he got back here just at dark. Bill, I hope Johnnie isn't in trouble. I tried to pump Sally, but all she did was set her jaw and work a little harder."

Before my imagination caught fire, and I swallowed some, I got busy and started to catch up on the ranch accounts. While I was trying to find out who won, me or the tax man, Al Neeman and Buck Bruen got all our tents, pack saddles, panniers, rope, and the rest of the hunting gear, slung up and stored away for the winter. We'd throwed all the horse and mule bunch in that good saved-up pasture below the creek. Getting ready to cut logs for some new cabins was next.

We just started to eat, and was all talking about beginning the log deal, when Pete Elaby came in through the kitchen, and Velma set another place for him. He said Wilson was sure lucky. Pete pulled in to the gas station for some fuel, and Slim caught a ride with a hunter going below in a truck to the town on the railroad. Pete took Shorty over to his cabin, helped the cook unload his gear, drove over to the store and post office to get the stuff for the ranch, had a bite and a cup of coffee at the greasy spoon, and came on home. "Dang road's sure glassy," he said, "and that snow comin' down sure looks like business. Winter's about ta ketch up with us. Woulda been back earlier, but that loggin' truck for th' sawmill in town was crosswise th' road fer awhile; sure slick travelin'. "

I kept quiet about Sally. That dog Moocher had a good house and was friendly, but I knew he'd have to move over if I said anything about the Sally-Johnnie rattles in my head. Velma's got a mother complex about both those kids, but I had that buzzing up above.

That night I was visiting with the boys over in the bunkhouse. We got to talking about the mystery of Johnnie and Sally, when Al Neeman spoke up. "I hope it ain't so, but I'll betcha Johnnie has fell fer some floozie in th' big town." "Happens alla time," says Buck, cutting the top off an old boot to make a staple bag. "Yeah, Johnnie workin' hard, an' lonely, probly met some swivel-hipped, eye-rollin' little tart on th' make. Yeah, hear it on th' radio' an' see it in th' papers any day o' th' week." Pete had it a little different but it ended up the same. "Well, I'm like you fellers, too, I think th' world o' them kids, but that's life, yuh gotta live yer own and God help you. Yessir, I can't help thinkin' about stoppin' by last summer, Bill. Stayed all night. I can't help rememberin' Johnnie playin' on his guitar an' Sally singin' with him. Th' tune they played was, 'The Sidewalks of New York.' "

What with building log cabins, ranch work, and odds and ends of things going on, we got back into a restful way of life in these hills. Buck, Pete, and Al got to see Shorty every time they went to town, and said he was really doing fine. They would razz him about his arthuritis and his youranium, but he claimed he'd planted some rich stuff under his cabin floor, and was gitting younger every day.

"Well, I seen Shorty in the Post Office when I got th' mail this afternoon," Buck said one evening. "He was lookin' sassier'n ever. He was mailin' a bundle of stuff, ta Johnnie in New York, I thought mebbe. But when he told Whiskers behind the bars that it was C.O.D., I peeked, and danged if it didn't say 'Smithers' on th' package!"

Damn! Did you say belly-wobblers? I'd visited with the cook a time or two, and thought all my suspicions was a hell of a reflection on an old friendship. Now, that squirmin' started all over again.

It kinda let up, but in a week or two, on a hell of a cold day, it started up again. I was in the old storehouse where we keep our gear; I was a-tryin' to ketch a pesky pack rat. I pulled down the cook tent,

99

all folded up on a rafter log. Damned if a couple of wadded up pieces of paper didn't fall out. Woulda thought they was lunch paper or somethin,' except they was covered all over with scribblin.' Looked like several tries at writing a letter. Couldn't tell whose it was. It was plenty cold in that building. The logs in the walls looked like big freckled horizontal icicles. Thirty-five below, the thermometer said that morning. But when I finally got the wrinkled papers outa them folds of canvas, and flattened out, and figgered out what they said, who from and who to, I got the tropical tantrums.

When I galloped outa that frigid log building, I was a-sweating like an amature bridegroom. Pete was a-warmin' up the pickup for a town trip, an' it was right in front of the bunkhouse, with a pan full o' hot coals under the oil pan. The steam and vapor round it looked like Niagery Falls to an old maid. I took me a runnin' jump inta that mumblin' gas wagon an' got her started. That hell-bent wheelspinnin' throwed me and that fool pickup around in a circle. I could see my wife lookin' out th' kitchen door, then Al, Buck an' Pete run outa th' bunkhouse t' watch th' crazy man. But I didn't have time for any damfool palaverin.' I was goin' t' town t' have it out with that connivin,' bandy-legged, grub-spoilin,' crooked old cook. Friend, hell.

As I was a-grittin' my teeth down that frozen, rutty old road, I looked in th' glass. Back there was the boys a-throwin' snow on the coals throwed into th' bunkhouse. One was holdin' th' run-over biscuit pan, and Velma was a-wavin' her hands up 'n' down alongside the snowdrift by th' house, an' I could see she was hollerin,' too—I dang near got stuck a time or two in them big drifts, crosswise th' road. —Why, damn that frosted windshield. —Shorty musta lost them tries at letter-writin'—probly thought he burned 'em up—somehow got caught in th' folds when we took down that cook tent. —Man, is this road skiddy—that letter t' Johnnie—that crooked stock deal, yeah— damn that moose an' her calf—always gotta git in th' road—so Smithers took th' kid fer his school stake—wouldn't yuh know it—I better watch her—comin' back now—Hay, yuh damn flop nosed fool!—jest dented the fender—If I git t' town without wreckin' this outfit, I'll be lucky—Damn kid tryin' t' increase his school money— dang near graduate dentist now—I guess that moose ain't hurt none— there, she an' her calf are goin' through th' timber—windshield foggin' up again—hope Pete put oil in this engine—yeah, Shorty tells Johnnie t' stay in school—damn that big-shot Smithers—so Shorty tells th' kid he'd make a deal—git th' money from that damn Full-pockets, come hell or high water, Shorty writes—Why, that damn crooked cook!—hope these ol' tires hold up—windshield foggin' up again, damn it—old friend, hell—hell—I'll fix that old so-and-so—Betcha Slim's in on this—them shots we heard—somethin' haywire about that mine hole deal—good thing I found them tries at letters—boy, it's a wonder I c'n stay on th' road—this zigzaggin' snow—damn him—his false teeth an' th' same kind o' friendship—that crooked ol' sharpie *couldn't* be killin' elk now—fer th' tusks—season's closed—or could he?—mebbe that dang galoot's arthuritis is a plum fake—an' that youranium!—damn—I hope I c'n make it t' town—that gas gauge sure is gittin' low—why'n hell do elk have t' have tusks anyhow?—I always tried t' run a square outfit—this's gotta happen—I have a good rep—I think—outfitter's license—bonded guide, too—for years—I'll give that crooked ol' youranium elk killer what he's got comin'—Damn that kinda friend—

The closer I got to Shorty's the madder I got. Take *me* for a sucker. I skidded past the gas station, but I figgered I better stop at Uncle Sam's an git th' mail right now. Because after I see that grub-spoilin' ol' mountain canary and give him what he's got comin', I'll be too wore out t' stop then or any other damn time.

I fumbled that two-bit ketch on the frustrated cab door open and stomped through the deep snow to the Post Office. I was reaching for the door knob, I was in a high lope by then, when some fool yazoo opened the door to come out. I missed that ding-danged knob, slipped on the icy board walk and fell flat. My drippy cold nose rested on one of the wet shoepacks of that toothtimin',' grub-spoilin',' mountain Methuselah, Shorty John Beel, his crooked old self! He reached down, got me by one outraged arm, pulled me up, and says, "Old Bill Thompson's a-hittin' th' mountan dew, shore as hell. Got a snootful, Bill?"

I shook that bent-up knobby old claw off my holy old mackinaw, and yowled, "Listen, you unnameable excuse of a fatherless old sidehill wampus, what I got ta say ta you won't work in this cheap emporium of Uncle Sam's. You just git on th' outside till I git my ding-danged miserable mail, and I'll fix your arthuritis without any antidose of that counterfeit youranium." I waltzed over to my box, yanked out my key, opened her up, and out fell two lonely hi-falutin-looking long envelopes. I looked out the steamed-up window, and that onery wrinkled-up old Shorty was tryin' t' peer in at the locoed packer, Bill Thompson, his former good friend.

Well, the first letter on that splintery old fir floor was marked *from*:

James (Slim) Wilson
Field Inspector
U. S. Game and Fish Comm.
Washington, D.C.
It was marked IMPORTANT.

The other one I turned over right quick, and caught that whiskery, small-time politician of an old postmaster a-peerin' out of his mangy cell, with his mouth open clear to his purple-green gizzard. I throwed him the right kinda glare and looked at th' top corner of this letter. It says plain: *from*

Mr. George Parsin
Chief Technician
Natural History Building
New York 92, N.Y.
It was also marked IMPORTANT.

I ripped the first one open, give her a quick goin' over, an' I dang near fainted right on them squeaky floor boards. Then I peeked out th' frosted-up window, and there was poor old Shorty, still standin' outside, slappin' his cold thin arms agin his sheepskin coat, an' stampin' his cold feet up an' down on the old board walk.

Then I jest had t' rip Parsin's letter open. What I saw quick there made me want to go suck onto that puffin' exhaust pipe of the chewed-up ol' pickup, still achuggin' out there on high priced gas. Then I jest had t' go over t' that window, that my good friend, that fine postmaster Whiskers O'Leary, was a-starin' out of, shake his suspicious and gentle old hand, and say, "I wasn't mayself, Whiskers, old friend. Next time I come t' town th' drinks are on me. Merry Christmas, old boy!"

I run out of that lovely old building of Uncle Sam's and grabbed my fine and cherished friend Shorty by his freezin' lonely old arms, and I be damned if I didn't hug that angelic old mountain purveyor of fine food and intellectual integrity.

But when I kissed him, damned if he didn't bust me between my miserable, close-together, dumb peepers. "Look out!" he yelped, "Yuh crazy counterfitten four flusher. Are yuh nuts? Mountain sickness agin. Why, DAMN YUH!"

"I got over bein' nuts, right in Whiskers' stamp shop just now," I said, and meant it. "Shorty, you wily ol' wolf, you are as of now elected chairman of the festive board, and you won't be the cook." He put up an argument, but I wore him down, and persuaded him to come up to the ranch for the holidays.

After he wrapped up his sourdough keg in a couple of blankets and started to take it down cellar, I throwed down them two letters on his bed, and told him to read them while I went over to town. Just as I started out the door, I said, "Shorty, it's sure tough that Johnnie and Sally busted up." "Whaddayuh mean, busted up?" Shorty came out of the cellar, keg and all, so fast some sourdough slopped out and hit him in the eye. He wiped it out with his fist without even noticing. "They're gonna git married right after Christmas! Sally's on her way t' New York right now. Johnnie's done with school in a month er two. Th' army's got him then an' Sally'll be with him." He set the keg down on the floor and reached over to the window sill. "Here, you dumb sap, take this along with you. Read it. It's a letter I stoled offa Sally last fall. I'll be ready when you come back."

While I'm still in a daze with the letter he hands me, I drove over to town and read it right quick. That envelope was post-marked New York City, too. It was from Johnnie by way of Sally, and was old, a couple months maybe. Was waterstained and kinda fuzzy.

Dearest Sally,

This is going to be hard to say, but we might as well call it quits—You never in the world should marry as big a fool as I've turned out to be. —Here it is, I may as well get it over with. When we made our plans to get married after I got my degree in dentistry, we figured that by another year we would be on our feet and be a going concern. Well, I thought I could speed it up by taking the advice of the big stocks-and-bonds hunter that Bill had out in camp when I was there last fall. Smithers is his name. Well, to make it short, he had a private talk with me, before he took off for the east after his hunt. He showed me a list of what he called confidential reports of several industrial ventures, just putting shares on the market. —Gilt-edge, he said—can't lose—get in on the ground floor—secret Government contracts about a new uranium process— hush-hush weapons manufactory—State Department friends in on the deal. He said that Uncle Shorty, Bill, and Velma, and the mountain people, were out of touch with the *real world outside*. Especially the business world. Why, he said, they don't even have television! "In the mountain country," he said, "living like your people do, they naturally wouldn't know how many ways there are to double your income and more, by taking advantage of the progress and rapid change in the outside world." He said he knew if he showed Uncle Shorty or Bill or Velma this group of confidential investment stock plans, they would just laugh at him. —Well, I thought it was hooey, too, until I got back here in school. I talked with some of my classmates, and showed them the list of big name investors. Several of them were very much impressed.

Well, a fool and his money are soon ——— that's me! I put the whole six thousand I had left in his confidential secret shares deal. Floated on air for awhile, and now WHAM!

So, to go on, I'm going to have to leave school. My tuition and living expenses are going to be due before long, and I'm broke.

Please, if you love me, don't tell Uncle Shorty or Bill or Velma what a stupid fool I've been. I have a chance to take a job in about 30 days as a purser, a sort of bookkeeper, aboard an oil ranker on the South American run. The wages are good, and maybe in another couple of years I can save up enough money to finally earn that degree as a dentist.

Please don't tell the folks what a jackass you let yourself get engaged to.

Sally, dearest, forget me and look for someone worthy of you.

Until now,
Your Johnnie.

(Part of letter from Slim Wilson) . . . And among other things, Bill, I did tell some white lies. That halter I kept tied to my saddle was to lead a relay horse, as I had to cover a lot of country in my investigations. The enclosed check is to pay for his use. I was in touch with state and government game men some of the time. I am happy to report to you that several unprincipled outfitters and some wanton game killers are in custody, awaiting trial.

In our books, you and your whole crew have the best A-1 Rating as outfitter and guides in your whole area. And, Bill, you paid me for the best vacation I ever had. I am now putting into effect some of the ideas and suggestions you and the boys unconsciously gave me, as to a game warden's real duties; and some on game management that are practical. The men will have to live more with the game and less with the people. I'll never forget one of old Buck's remarks: "Some of our game wardens are people wardens. They know a damn sight more about people than they do about game."

And, Bill, please give my affectionate regards to Buck, Al, and Pete, and especially to that good old pal of mine, Shorty. He is a fine cook, an expert mountain man, and is sure handy with his fingers. Did that old boy have me fooled! Those extra rifle shots!

104

Please ask him to forgive me for being a snoop. I looked over those false-elk-teeth molds he had cached away. Best counterfeits I ever saw. That dental office he had in Tinsley's old prospect sure fits the country. Some day I am going to come out and have a hunt with the best outfit I know of, if you'll let me.

Please give my best regards to Mrs. Thompson, and have some yourself, Bill. And when you see her, my best to litle Sally. Merry Christmas to a fine outfit.

From your friend, the "sneaky" horse wrangler,
James (Slim) Wilson

(Part of Parsin's letter) . ... What you'll be most interested in, Bill, is a party at Tim Smithers' sportsman's club. He invited me, and I'm glad I went. A bunch of his hunter friends were gathered around him admiring his coat—the one he bragged about getting made, with 1000 elk teeth to adorn it. Well, Bill, there it was. A beautiful white buckskin, Indian-made coat. It was really decorated! We all admired it, handed it round, tried it on, and so forth. While a big young man about Smithers' size was admiring it, he remarked to Tim, "Man, I'd sure love to have this." Smithers said it wasn't quite complete, "I need one elk tooth to make up the thousand. It should be here tonight." Well, would you believe it, about that time a messenger came in with a special delivery package for Smithers. He signed and paid for it. Then he opened it with a big flourish. But when he read the note enclosed, he seemed to shrink, then I thought our big friend was going to have a heart attack. He dropped *two* elk teeth out of the box on to the table, threw the note on the floor, and stood up. He was flushed up like one of your beautiful Wyoming sunsets. But he wasn't pretty: he was mad, and trembling like a quaking aspen leaf. He said in a raspy little voice to the young man who'd "love to have this:" "Take the coat, my friend. It's all yours, as of now!" Then he stomped out the closest door. I heard him mumbling as he went out: "Oh, that smart damn sucker! Oh, that smart damn sucker!" And, Bill, did he slam that big oak door! The crowd stood watching Smithers' exit, so I picked up the note, and here is what was on it: "inclosed is a extry unfinished false tooth to show how they was all made. Thanks for th cash. Let the punishment fit the crime. So long, sucker. From the Country Wolf."

I am enclosing five sets of colored pictures I took around camp. Please give one set each to Buck, Al, Shorty, and Slim. One set is for you, Bill. I also enclose a good one of Pete and his pack string, which I hope he likes. Doctor Forrester and I plan on a trip with you and the boys next fall, about which you'll be hearing from us soon. My best regards to you and all the boys, and the pretty Shoshone girl, Sally. Please give my best to your fine wife, Mrs. Thompson.

Merry Christmas to you all,
Your friend, George Parsin.

Well! By th' Jaysus! For *one* time I'm gonna fall off the wagon. So I drove that faithful pickup over to the right place, and got a jug of the best. Then I got a couple of the fattest turkeys they had at the store, and all the fixins, and a tankful of gas for the chariot. When I got back to the cabin, Shorty was sitting on the bed with a big grin on his wrinkled old mug. He had his best clothes on, all ready to go. He handed me the incriminating letters and pushed me out of the door.

He says, "Let's go home, sucker."

Joe Back was born in Ohio in 1899 and moved to Wyoming when he was thirteen. He served as a machine gun instructor during World War I, then took up trade as a cowboy, guide, and packer. Later he spent four years at the Art Institute of Chicago where, to use Joe's words, he "damn near starved to death." Art education changed his life, however, and although he went back to packing and guiding, he also became nationally known as a sculptor. Joe Back died September 7, 1986 at age 87—through the magic of his illustrations and writing we celebrate and share his work.